"For you," Ray said. "And with it, my heart."

Cami reached for  d
opened it. Inside e
satin, twinkled a a
platinum band.

"Say you'll say yes…" Ray murmured.

Drawing back, Cami pressed trembling hands to her cheeks. Though she'd dreamed of this moment, the reality was so scary that she hesitated. She couldn't say yes. But she didn't want to say no.

In Ray, she'd met a man she desired, respected, trusted and loved. Someone who offered her the commitment she demanded as the price for her innocence…

She inhaled a deep breath and let it out slowly while contemplating him. He seemed so sincere.

I want to care for you all the days of my life, he had said. She couldn't have asked for a sweeter proposal.

"Yes," she whispered. Then, more boldly, "Yes! Yes! Yes!"

A criminal defence attorney for twenty years, **Sue Swift** always sensed a creative wellspring bubbling inside her, but didn't find her niche until attending a writing class with master teacher Bud Gardner. Within a short time, Sue realised her creative outlet was romance fiction. The 2001 president of the Sacramento Chapter of the Romance Writers of America, Sue credits the RWA, its many wonderful programmes and the help of its experienced writers for her new career as a romance novelist. She also lectures to women's and writers groups on various topics related to the craft of writing.

Her hobbies are hiking, bodysurfing and kenpo karate, in which she's earned a second degree black belt. Sue and her real-life hero of a husband maintain homes in northern California and Maui, Hawaii. Please visit Sue's website: www.sue-swift.com

IN THE
SHEIKH'S ARMS

BY
SUE SWIFT

MILLS & BOON®

This book is dedicated to Barbara McMahon,
who inspired it.

First published in Great Britain 2006
Paperback Edition 2006
Harlequin Mills & Boon Limited,
Eton House, 18-24 Paradise Road, Richmond, Surrey TW9 1SR

© Susan Freya Swift 2003

ISBN 0 263 84807 8

Set in Times Roman 10½ on 12½ pt.
01-0406-39787

Printed and bound in Spain
by Litografia Rosés, S.A., Barcelona

Prologue

Ten years ago

Fury raging in his heart, Rayhan ibn-Malik stomped on the accelerator. His Land Rover surged forward, churning clouds of Texas dust as he left his spread, the Double Eagle. He drove at a wild pace in through the Ellisons' open gate.

Nothing had changed at the C-Bar-C since Rayhan had put his name to the deceptive deed and purchased the Double Eagle. No hint of scandal seething beneath the broad plains. No trace of the oil riches bubbling under the surface of this peaceful ranch.

No clue to reveal the wealth Rayhan thought he'd purchased from Charles Ellison. No sign of the bounty the old man had promised.

The C-Bar-C appeared as calm and well managed as ever. Oil pumps and derricks punctuated the distant horizon. A line of trees bordered the stream meandering between the two ranches. Orderly corrals penned the Ellisons' stock.

Rayhan's heartbeat tripled as he passed the stable, nearing the main house. Brief days ago he'd relaxed in that white, balconied home, sipping beer and signing documents in apparent friendship with Charles Ellison.

Bitterness twisted Rayhan's gut. In all fairness, he couldn't entirely blame Ellison. Rayhan's own poor English and incompetent attorney had doubtless contributed to the debacle...in part.

But only in part.

Rayhan jerked the steering wheel to the left, avoiding a circle of lawn set in the middle of the wide, graveled drive. Pebbles sprayed from beneath the tires. He stamped on the brake, bringing the Rover to a halt.

As if Rayhan had been expected, Ellison waited on the veranda. Rayhan couldn't discern the older man's expression in the shadows. Getting out of the Rover, Rayhan slammed its door behind him. With no reason to censor his words, he said, "You cheated me."

Ellison smiled. But the twitch of his lips wasn't triumphant. Worse, the old man appeared patronizing. "Next time, you'll read closer, pup. A cheap lesson. You'll never get suckered again."

Rayhan flushed. *Pup.* At age twenty, he didn't need reminders of his inexperience. "Again? What again? That worthless transaction took all my money."

Ellison shrugged. "You got a fine ranch, and a beautiful herd of Herefords to boot."

"Cows?" Rayhan snorted. "Cows, and none of the oil that flows beneath the land." Without the oil riches he craved, Rayhan would have nothing to show his family in Adnan. No way to prove to his father, the king, that Rayhan was worthy of the government post he wanted and knew he deserved. A younger son, he'd long accepted he would never rule, but he yearned for the power, responsibility and respect he had earned through his birth and education.

"I couldn't sell you the mineral rights even if I wanted to. They belong to her." Old Man Ellison nodded in the direction of the patch of lawn in the middle of the drive.

Rayhan hadn't previously noticed the scruffy young girl kneeling on the grass, playing with a litter of puppies. The child's blond hair, crookedly parted, was bound into two awkward plaits. With green grass stains marring her pink overalls, the girl's unkempt appearance startled Rayhan. Nannies and nurses had always kept his sisters immaculate. This ragamuffin was a wealthy oil magnate?

Through his surprise and wrath, Rayhan struggled to grasp the situation. "The oil belongs to this child?"

"My daughter, Camille." Ellison's chest swelled with obvious pride. He walked down the porch steps and past Rayhan, who still stood on the graveled drive. The old man joined the child on the grass, continuing to speak.

"This here land belonged to her mother's family. That's why it's called the C-Bar-C, for the Crowells. My wife left everything to Cami. I manage it, of course. By the terms of the will, I could sell you the land, but not the oil rights. When she's an adult, it'll all be hers."

Rayhan's gaze locked onto the fair-haired child. Raising her head, she stared back with wide blue eyes. Thank heaven for little girls, he thought, mentally paraphrasing an old song. For they'll grow up into vulnerable young women.

Rayhan smiled. It'll all be hers, Ellison had said.

No, old man. It'll all be mine.

Chapter One

Cami Ellison stood in front of her bathroom mirror, brushing her long hair with frustrated strokes. She glowered at her reflection as though the fierceness of her stare could zap the zit on her chin out of existence. *Nearly twenty and I still have skin like a thirteen-year-old!*

After throwing her brush onto the pink-tiled counter with a clatter, she spread sunscreen on her face and concealer over the pimple. She plaited her hair into a braid that fell below her shoulders. After securing it with a purple scrunchie, she flung open the door of her closet to survey the contents.

A strange restlessness consumed her. She wanted something—anything—to happen, like a con eagerly awaiting a planned escape. She knew her widowed father had spoiled her, but after a year away at college, Cami felt caged by the routine dullness of life with Dad on the C-Bar-C Ranch.

Since her return from San Antonio, armed with new knowledge from her studies, she'd spent every day running the ranch. But today...if she didn't get out of the house she'd start to beat her head against the walls.

She didn't know what she wanted but, jumpy and tense, she sure did want something. Maybe a good hard ride would get rid of the tension coiling in her belly, so tight and sharp it was a physical need, an ache she'd never before felt and one that she didn't know how to soothe.

She pulled on a sports bra, then covered it with a T-shirt. Tugging on stretch jeans, she tucked the pink top into her pants, then cinched on a tooled leather belt. She shoved her feet into battered cowboy boots and grabbed her old Stetson from its perch on a hook above her desk.

Though Cami loved her father and their long-time housekeeper, Robbie, the thought of exchanging pleasantries with them over coffee and toast made her want to scream. She skipped breakfast, hurrying out of the house and heading directly to the stables.

At the entrance she breathed deeply and calmed herself, at least a fraction, her shoulders settling lower and her heartbeat slowing. The warmth of the stable, the late June sunlight slanting in through its high windows and its familiar animal smells all reminded her of her childhood.

She paced down the row of stalls, greeting old friends, until she came to her buddy, Sugar. Sugar, a palomino mare, had been her mount since Cami's teenage growth spurt had retired Funnyface, her pony.

Cami opened the stall door and Sugar started forward. She tucked her long nose against Cami's shoulder to snort a greeting, as she did every day Cami lived at the C-Bar-C. Laughing, Cami caught Sugar's bridle to lead her in the direction of the tack room.

A few minutes later they were cantering across the C-Bar-C's fields. A line of bushes and trees shimmered, gray-green and dusty, in the distance. Cami remembered that their foliage hid a winding stream that divided the C-Bar-C from the Double Eagle, Ray Malik's horse farm.

The gossips in the nearby town, McMahon, said that Malik's Arabians, valued as studs and mares, had won numerous prizes, including an Olympic medal for dressage. Though they'd been neighbors for ten years, Cami didn't know Ray personally. Her father, who maintained friendships with just about everyone, had always kept his distance from Ray Malik. He'd never shared his reasons for snubbing Malik with Cami, and Cami, sensitive to her elderly father's feelings, had never asked.

Cami and Sugar entered the dappled shade of the cottonwoods bordering the stream. Cami loosened her hold on the reins, allowing Sugar her head. The mare picked her way to the water, stopping where the creek widened into a hidden swimming hole. She dropped her head and drank from the quiet pond.

After sliding off her horse's back, Cami leaned against a convenient tree to stretch her quads and hamstrings. Though an experienced rider, she hadn't been on horseback for months—not since her previous visit home. She was tight.

Through the branches, she glimpsed a flash of white fabric billowing in the breeze, Cami craned her head around the mare to see better, absentmindedly stroking Sugar's rough mane.

A rider on a big, gray horse entered the thicket alongside the creek. Catching a look at his white, fluttering head scarf, Cami wondered who on earth wore such bizarre attire. While a cynical part of her thought he looked like a refugee from an old Rudolph Valentino flick, her romantic soul was titillated by the Arabian headdress floating in the breeze.

He'd slowed the beautiful gray to a stop between the cottonwoods, allowing his horse to refresh itself in the water. Cami and her mare remained hidden behind a clump of bushes.

The man dismounted. Removing his headgear and a white shirt, he bared himself to the waist above tan jodhpurs and riding boots. His body, slick and burnished by sweat, gleamed bronze in the golden morning sunlight.

Cami's breath stuck somewhere in her throat. She pulled off her Stetson and used it to fan herself. She'd seen a man's naked torso, of course, but none of her classmates had ever struck her as…beautiful.

The man had to be Ray Malik, their mysterious neighbor. His years of hard work breeding and training Arabians showed in his broad shoulders and sinewy pecs. He knelt beside the creek, splashing the cool water onto his face and neck. When he shook his head, his longish hair scattered crystalline drops in an arc, glittering in the light.

How would he feel? Cami wondered. She'd never

stroked a man's nude chest. Now she imagined running her fingertips along those sculptured planes, rimming his dark nipples with her nails.

Her hand involuntarily clenched in Sugar's mane. Her mare shied away, snorting, then backed away from the stream, exposing Cami.

The man jerked upright. His gaze, palpable as a touch, fastened on her. Intent eyes assessed her with the attitude of a sheikh selecting a slave girl for the night. Then he smiled, gesturing for her to cross the stream onto his land.

Cami hesitated, mindful of her father's distant attitude toward Ray. On the other hand, Charles Ellison had never overtly warned her away from Ray or forbidden her to set foot on the Double Eagle.

And she'd been curious about Ray Malik for as long as she could remember. Over the years she occasionally glimpsed him in McMahon and around his ranch, mounted on one of his gorgeous Arabians. She'd heard intriguing rumors about him.

The more outlandish storytellers said that he was an Arab prince exiled from his family because of his politics. Others said he'd been a spy, now retired to this quiet corner of Texas. Some gossiped about his trysts, though none of the exotic women he was rumored to bed ever appeared in McMahon.

Well, she'd wanted something to happen. An old proverb rolled through her mind. "Be careful what you wish for...you might get it."

Cami gathered Sugar's reins, then remounted. Clicking her tongue against her teeth, she guided the mare to a narrow ford, then urged her across the stream.

Heat rose in her cheeks, but she didn't know how to hide her embarrassment. This wildly attractive male had caught her spying on him. An older man, he radiated sensuality and experience. She felt young and absurdly unsophisticated by comparison.

However, she wanted to capture his interest, prove she could attract a man more mature and worldly than the boys she'd dated in high school and college.

Cami knew she was playing with fire. Seduction wasn't on her agenda, but she realized that a man as handsome as Ray Malik probably expected more than pleasant conversation from a woman who flirted with him. She told herself not to promise anything she didn't intend to deliver.

She was honest enough to admit that although she wanted his attention, she didn't know how to get it. "Do you come here often?" or "What's your sign?" wouldn't cut the mustard. Nor would the usual opening lines that worked on campus. "What classes are you taking?" just didn't make sense here. But what did?

Cami watched the spot between Sugar's ears, the glittering water as it splashed from the mare's hooves…anything to avoid Ray's dark, keen stare.

Sugar came to the bank of the creek. She climbed the shore, and Cami halted her mount beside Ray's. She raised her gaze to meet his.

Rich and brown, his eyes glinted with a roguish humor. She was close enough to catch his scent, a spicy aftershave that hinted at mysterious souks and exotic ports of call. None of which, she glumly reminded herself, she had ever seen.

She was *such* a zero. How could she hope to interest a man like Ray Malik?

She cleared her throat. "Hi. Uh, I'm Cami, and this is Sugar," she blurted like a dork.

He smiled. Even, white teeth gleamed against his stubbly cheek. His skin was the color of wildflower honey. He had a beautiful mouth, with lips that weren't too thin or too puffy, topped by a totally adorable Cupid's bow. Her tummy did flip-flops, becoming all warm and squishy.

"I know who you are, Camille Crowell Ellison. And I know of your Sugar. She's a lovely mare. She has very good bloodlines." He stroked her horse's neck, and Sugar responded with a friendly chuff.

Cami's surprise at Ray's knowledge of her full true name was overshadowed by his interest in her beloved Sugar. "How do you know?"

"I know everything about you."

She nearly fell out of the saddle. "Why? How? No one can know everything about another person."

"I have watched you for many years."

She should have been creeped out. Wasn't he admitting he was a stalker or a Peeping Tom? On the other hand, she'd been the one spying on him as he cooled off in the water. "Why?"

"It is hard for me not to be interested in a pretty young woman, especially one who rides almost as well as do I." Ray winked at her.

She gasped. Cami, a veteran of many riding competitions, wasn't about to take a back seat to anyone—certainly not if the seat was on a horse. "Even if you do say so yourself." She was determined to deflate this man's massive ego.

His impish grin made his dark eyes twinkle. She could have sworn he was out to get her goat. But why?

"No insult intended, as you Americans might say. I am pulling your leg." Ray reached for her ankle, seizing it with one big hand. He gave it a gentle tug.

Even through her boot, she felt his strong grasp. His power remained controlled, so he didn't haul her off her mount. She figured he could have if he'd wanted. But he didn't.

What was this man's game?

She looked down at him. He released her foot, then strolled to the pile of white cloth he'd left when he'd partially stripped. He slid his arms into his shirt, allowing it to remain open at the chest, then arranged his headdress. His muscles rippled beneath satiny, amber skin.

Cami pulled her shirt away from her chest to cool down. "What's with the head thingie?" she asked.

He shrugged. "Occasionally, I miss my country, so I will dress in the garb of my people. It is very comfortable. Wrapped correctly, my *gutra* will keep dust out of my face quite well. Have you ever worn one?"

"N-no."

He gathered his horse's reins, then vaulted into the saddle in one smooth, elegant motion.

Cami had to admit to herself that she'd never mastered that little trick. "Nice horse. One of your Arabians?"

"I haven't told you who I am." His grin turned wicked.

She sniffed. "You're not the only one who knows the neighborhood. You're Ray Malik. You raise Arabians at the Double Eagle."

"Ah, so you know all about me." Rayhan sincerely hoped not. If her father had poisoned her ears with tales about Ray's anger at the oil swindle, he'd never have a chance to fulfill his long-planned revenge.

Over the years Rayhan had been careful to avoid Charles Ellison. He didn't want Ellison to have any reason to gossip to his daughter about the rancher next door. Since the disastrous land deal, Rayhan had done nothing more remarkable than raise horses and travel.

He wanted to alter the course of the conversation, and remembered a compliment always worked on women. "You sit your mare very well. Have you competed?"

She actually blushed and ducked her head. What was wrong with American males? This stunning young woman behaved as though no one ever praised her. Impossible. Ridiculous. However, Rayhan liked her modesty.

Her shirt and jeans revealed a curvy, feminine body. She still had pale hair, a mane gleaming like a halo in the morning sun. It was bound into a long, tidy braid which draped over her shoulder and curled around one round breast, like a lover's caress. He envied that braid.

Rayhan smiled. The ragamuffin had grown into a princess. Revenge would be sweet indeed.

"Yeah," she said. "Sugar and I used to compete before I went away to college in San Antonio. I don't have time to ride when I'm at school."

"San Antonio's a nice town. What classes are you taking?"

Cami's eyes widened. Her hands tightened on the reins, jerking them. For no reason Rayhan could fathom, the question seemed to astound her. Her mount turned her large head to give Cami the equine equivalent of a steely glare.

"Have a care," he said. "You sit your mare well, but she doesn't like quick movements."

"I know that. You surprised me, that's all."

"Why?"

"Your question about my classes."

"As I said, it is not unusual for a man to be interested in a pretty woman, especially if she lives on the ranch next door." Odd that Cami didn't grasp the basics about male-female relationships. Could she be such an innocent?

"You never showed any interest before."

"You were too young. A man who is friendly with a young girl is…gross, as you Americans might say."

She laughed. "I guess you're right. Well, to answer your question, I'm studying business, specifically oil."

"So, you know what you wish to do?"

"Oh, I want to stay here." Cami sounded definite. "The C-Bar-C is my home. I'll run the family oil business. I've been helping my dad for years."

"What if you married?" he asked, keeping his voice even.

"What if I did? My husband better like Texas, that's all I can say."

Rayhan decided he'd like Texas long enough to get what—or rather who—he wanted. He showed her his teeth. "Then it is fortunate indeed that I like Texas."

Confusion drifted over Cami's face before she managed a nervous smile. Rayhan realized he was moving too fast, and that he'd better back off.

"How do you jump into the saddle like that? Sugar won't let me."

She'd changed the subject, a sign she wanted to go slower. All right, he'd comply. If he could.

"It is easy, but your horse must expect the sudden weight. Try mounting Kalil." He slid out of his saddle.

"Wow, thanks." Cami dismounted and approached Kalil, stroking his nose. "He's gorgeous. Did you breed him?"

She'd drawn closer, now standing mere inches away. He inhaled her subtle fragrance. She didn't wear heavy perfume, so nothing artificial cloaked her natural, feminine aroma. He liked that. Her scent recalled the wind and the sky. Her eyes were the color of heaven.

Bedding her would be no chore.

With difficulty Rayhan reminded himself of his goal: revenge, not pleasure. He wrenched his mind back to their conversation. What had they been talking about? Ah, yes. Kalil. "Yes, he is one of my stock. I recognized early he would not be suitable for stud, so I gelded him and he has become my favorite saddle horse."

"Poor Kalil."

He laughed. "You must know that stallions make poor mounts. They are too wild and restless. You would not enjoy, for example, riding Karim, my prime stud. He would throw you into the dust in a matter of moments."

"Karim and Kalil. What do those names mean?"

"Karim means noble one, and Kalil is best friend."

"That's beautiful." Cami was entranced. The reality of Ray Malik was better than the rumors. He was handsome, he was nice and he said straight out that he was interested in her. No games. Cami liked that. She didn't like game players and she hated deception.

"So try jumping into the saddle. The trick is to use your thigh muscles."

Cami eyed Kalil. She was sure of the gelding's good manners, but he was a tall animal, at least seventeen hands. Though she wasn't short, she didn't know if she could leap into the saddle with Ray's grace. Now that he'd showed interest in her, she didn't want to mess things up by falling on her butt into the mud by the stream. "Maybe some other time."

"You are a scaredy-cat?"

Cami giggled. The child's phrase sounded hilariously incongruous coming from Ray's lips. "Am not!"

"Are too." He leaned against Kalil and regarded her from beneath lowered lids.

Bedroom eyes. That was what Ray had: bedroom eyes. Cami had never quite understood that phrase until this moment, when his smoldering glance had caught hers. She jerked her gaze away from his and fought for her fleeting poise. "You're…you're ridiculous."

"You are not up to a challenge."

With that outrageous statement, she recovered herself. "Of all the nerve! I can do anything you can do and better."

"Well, then. Let us try something less challenging but perhaps more exciting."

She turned and looked into his eyes. He stood close enough to touch, with his loose, white shirt hanging open to expose his muscular torso. He was virility personified.

Too close, too fast. Cami, don't promise what you can't deliver. She stepped back, sucking in an uneasy breath.

Mistake. His scent compelled her to draw nearer. She fought his pheromones and her instincts.

He smiled.

She was lost.

Ray ran a long, elegant finger along her jawline. Cami's flesh tingled; the tiny hairs along her skin rose. Closing her eyes, she inhaled, exquisitely aware of his exotic scent and her body. He'd somehow transformed her into a quivering mass of sensation with just one touch.

How had he done this? she wondered. She'd been touched before, but no other man had turned her on. With only one gentle stroke of the finger, Ray fanned her feminine fires into a blaze.

Her nipples rasped against the soft cups of her bra.

She didn't need to look down to see what had happened, and didn't want to. Burning with embarrassment and desire right down to her soul, she'd freak out if Ray noticed.

Part of her wanted to leave, but she couldn't let go of the challenge Ray had issued. She lifted her gaze to his.

Ray's glance shifted to her mouth, lingering there. He said, ''Have you ever kissed a man on horseback?''

Chapter Two

"Sure I have."

Anger surged through Rayhan. That another man had touched his Texan princess infuriated him. She was his.

He tamped down his outrage, reminding himself that she was an American girl. Many were casual about their couplings, even loose. She's probably had sex in the saddle, he thought with disgust. His gut twisted. Could he actually marry such a female, even to seize the fortune he deserved?

Honor must be cleansed. Revenge would bring great joy, but harnessing himself to used goods repelled him.

He looked at Cami. A faraway dreaminess had entered her eyes. "When I was a little girl, my daddy would put me in front of him and we'd ride every morning."

Rayhan relaxed. She'd cuddled with her father on horseback, not the college football team. "I have in mind something more…stimulating. Get on Sugar, and I'll show you." Mounting Kalil, he urged his horse alongside hers so they stood close.

Face to face with Cami, who was now back in Sugar's saddle, Rayhan could see a sparkling, feminine interest in her eyes. Taking a deep breath, he dropped Kalil's reins. His well-trained gelding stood rock still.

Rayhan reached for her, knowing he took a huge risk. He chanced spooking his prey. Though she shouldn't be pushed, he couldn't resist the open curiosity in her gaze. His quarry was within his grasp.

"Cami." He stroked her cheek, smooth and soft as the petals of a desert rose.

Her lips parted. He sensed her anticipation, her acceptance.

Leaning forward in his saddle, he touched his mouth to hers. Moist she was, and sweet. Better, she kissed him back with unmistakable innocence. Was it possible she'd remained untouched?

Rayhan's blood heated at the thought. He wanted more from her and took it.

Cami's world spun. She reached out and grabbed the open halves of Ray's shirt, seeking to steady herself. But deep inside she knew he didn't offer stability. Quite the contrary. He offered life in all of its tumult.

She'd been sheltered by her father's affection, but

now she hungered for another kind of love, the whirl-wind of falling for a potent, sexy male.

She would walk across Texas barefoot to have Ray.

Using his shirt to pull him closer, she responded when he deepened the kiss. He rubbed his thumbs along her jaw, urging her mouth open, then slid his tongue inside, penetrating her.

After one shocked, startled moment, the embers of her sexuality leaped into riotous flame. She burned from the inside out. She knew what she was doing was wrong, crazy, that Ray couldn't possibly be right for her. He'd demand more than she, a virgin, was prepared to give any man until she had a ring on her finger.

And yet, just one kiss from Ray caused her to question her deepest beliefs.

His lips curled sensuously around hers, and his tongue danced inside her mouth. She'd been kissed before, even Frenched, but the tentative caresses of the boys she knew had never felt like this. She'd never liked guys who slobbered all over her.

But Ray…Ray was different. He wasn't tentative, and he didn't slobber.

Stopping was out of the question.

Continuing was wrong, wrong, wrong. If they didn't quit, she'd let Ray sweep her away on a magic carpet of lust, and she'd give it up to him in the mud of the riverbank.

Sugar pranced back, snorting. Cami realized that her indecision must have communicated itself to her sensitive, intelligent mare.

Ray blinked at Cami. *"'Azhib."*

"If that means wow in Arabic, I gotta agree. That was some kiss."

He nodded slowly, heavy lids lifting over those sultry bedroom eyes. His expression was predatory, determined. He reached for her again.

It was now or never. Moistening her lips, Cami leaned back into her saddle, away from the temptation he offered. "I, uh, I think you should know that I don't do…that."

He dropped his hand. "Do what? Kiss a man?" He didn't sound surprised; in fact, he seemed as though he knew by her hesitation that she wasn't very experienced.

Embarrassment turned her body into one giant hot flash. "Do, you know…it."

"It?" Now he appeared genuinely puzzled.

Good heavens, she thought. Do I have to spell everything out? Then, remembering their cultural and language barriers, she concluded, probably.

She swallowed, and, making an effort to be absolutely clear and totally honest, said, "I don't sleep around with men."

A pause ensued. "That is something of a relief," he finally said, in English as precise and careful as hers. "That kiss would be less special if you did. But why is this, Cami?" His words quickened. "You are, what, twenty years of age? I remember what it was like to be so young."

"Like you're so old. And I'm nineteen."

He grimaced as though the news were unwelcome. "I was twenty when I came to Texas a decade ago."

"Wow. So you're thirty?" She sagged. "Dad'll flip out."

"You are right." Again, Ray seemed to choose his words carefully. "Your father, he may not approve of me."

"Why not?"

"I am much older than are you. To be truthful, I should not be with you at all." He turned his horse away, as if preparing to leave.

"Wait!" Cami urged her mare forward, blocking his path. "See here, I'm an adult. My father knows that I'll see who I want."

"You sound like a very disobedient daughter. This is not good. I would not cause a rift in your family." Ray's nose crinkled, giving him a comically disapproving look.

She had to smile. "Listen, I'm not going to do anything wrong. I told you, I don't...you know."

"You made this decision though other girls, um, do it?"

Cami shifted her weight. "When I was in high school, my dad watched me pretty closely. And he made me promise not to do it until I turned eighteen. He said after I went to college I was an adult and could make my own decisions." She raised her gaze to Ray's. "I keep my promises."

"And now? Are you not nineteen and released from your vow?"

"Yeah, but when I went away to school, I saw all these girls jumping into the sack with guys they barely knew just to see what it was like."

"It? Sleep around?" His eyebrows drew together into a straight, dark bar.

"Yeah, you know, sex." She shrugged. "And it didn't make them happier. Some got pregnant and had to have abortions. Some got STDs—sexually transmitted diseases. Some had to drop out because they were so distracted by their boyfriends that they failed classes."

"So you decided not to—how can I say it—not to take that route?"

"Right." She bobbed her head up and down.

Rayhan couldn't have been more pleased. "I think you are a very smart woman, Cami Ellison." Confident he'd seduce her, he now knew she'd be a pristine vessel for his pleasure.

He glanced at her again, taking in the details he'd missed earlier. A determined little chin. A firm mouth. Both spoke of her strong will. This woman wouldn't be easy, but she'd be worth every second of effort it took to win her.

Cornsilk hair and bluebonnet eyes—his heartbeat quickened. He'd been in America long enough to widen his tastes in women beyond the petite, dark females of Adnan. He'd come to admire American girls in all their marvelous variety.

And Cami was a Texan princess, tall, strong, smart and untouched by any other. She was perfect.

More than a little surprised, Rayhan realized that his calculations hadn't taken into account the possibility that he might actually desire Ellison's daughter.

But it didn't matter. He'd have her, whatever.

He'd tested her by suggesting that her father might not approve of their liaison; she'd reacted with a show of independence. Cami was willing to risk her father's displeasure. She was ready.

"When will I see you again?" he asked, his voice oddly husky. He cleared his throat.

Her lashes fluttered. "You're seeing me now."

"Alas, I cannot tarry with you all day." Pushing back his cuff, he glanced at his watch. "I have a ranch to manage. But tonight—tonight is another matter. Do you enjoy dancing?"

"Sure."

"Do you know Dancin' Nancy's, in McMahon?"

"Yeah."

"Come to me tonight, at about nine."

Cami's body brightened with delight. She practically danced in the saddle. Her little bounce up and down startled Sugar, who gave Cami another glare.

He'd asked her out! On a date!

With a wrench, Cami turned her mind back to the practicalities of the situation, remembering her zit and her wardrobe. Later in the week her pimple might recede. Plus, she'd have a chance to go shopping. "How about, um, Saturday?"

"I'd rather see you sooner, but Saturday is all right, too." His smile made her dizzy. He touched the side of his hand to his forehead in a mock salute. "Saturday at nine, then."

* * *

Fortunately for Cami, her salon in San Antonio had done a decent job on her face. Attired in a new outfit—a blue cotton dress with a gathered peasant neckline, belted waist and ruffled hem—Cami sat at the bar in Dancin' Nancy's on Saturday night. Ray had said nine, but Cami, jumpy and anxious, had arrived early. She figured she'd have a soda and a couple of dances before he came, just so she wouldn't be so nervous.

She kicked the toes of her favorite dress boots—black-and-white spotted calf—against the polished wood bar. A large doughnut shape, the bar occupied the center of Dancin' Nancy's. On one side of the bar a group of pool tables sat beneath hanging Tiffany-style lamps. Cowboys and oil-field roughnecks, cigarettes hanging from their lips and mugs of beer at hand, shot pool and goofed off.

A country-western band was playing on the stage that stretched the length of the other side of the room. A dance floor, where Nancy herself gave lessons, filled the area between the stage and the bar. Colored stage lights glittering off a mirror ball lit the dance floor, ringed with booths.

Cami had been coming to Dancin' Nancy's since she was a teenager. Now, seated at the bar, she listened to the ebb and flow of chatter while thinking about Ray Malik.

She had to admit to herself that little else had occupied her mind for days. She longed for his touch, craved his kiss every conscious hour. When she slept, she dreamed of loving him.

Contemplating the bubbles rising in her soda, she realized she knew little about this mysterious man.

He wasn't an American.

He was thirty years old.

He raised great horses.

He was the most intriguing person she'd ever met, and she wanted to know more about him.

Cami heard his name as though it echoed her thoughts. She raised her gaze from her glass, startled.

Around the circular bar from Cami's seat, two women were talking about Ray, their voices barely audible above the music. Cami hesitated. Then, taking her glass, she moved two seats closer. Now her back was to the door so she couldn't see who entered, but she could hear mighty fine.

One of the women, a striking redhead in a black sequined top, was finishing her story. "And he put her on a plane in Houston and never saw her again."

"A supermodel?" Her companion's eyes widened into big green lily pads. "Gone, just like that?" She snapped her fingers.

Cami shrank back into her bar stool. Yikes. This man tossed away beautiful women like empty soda cans.

She craned her head to hear more, but one of the gossips caught sight of her. After they made eye contact, the other woman turned her back and lowered her voice.

But Cami had eavesdropped enough. She repeated to herself, Don't promise what you won't deliver!

Cami heard the door behind her open. A rush of

air raised the skin on her bare arms, even though the evening was warm and humid.

Ray had arrived.

She turned her head as he slid into the seat beside her. Her heart beat against the walls of her chest like a wild bird's wings. Across the bar, the chatterboxes fell silent. Cami couldn't stop herself from giving them a tiny, triumphant smile before devoting her full attention to Ray.

Tonight he wore jeans and a chambray workshirt, like many in the bar, but Ray stood out. His shirt was immaculate and pressed. Freshly washed, damp tendrils of dark hair coiled appealingly over his collar in tiny, cute curlicues. She caught his exotic scent when he leaned close to her and breathed into her ear, "Hello, Cami."

Playing with a lock of her loose hair, he said, "I like your hair unbound. It looks...wild and free."

Cami's mouth went dry. She swallowed, hoping he'd gotten the message when they'd last talked. He made her want to be wild and free, though at her own pace. Was that inconsistent? Probably, but Cami didn't care.

Ray leaned his forearms on the bar, exposing his wrists. One was circled by an expensive-looking gold watch.

Expensive was good, Cami thought. That meant he had money, so he wasn't after the C-Bar-C. When she turned fourteen, her father had started to warn her about boys who would want her for the ranch.

The sight of Ray's long-fingered, strong hands reminded Cami of the feel of those warm palms on her face when they'd kissed. Her heart tripped at the memory.

That had been the most thrilling moment of her life. She breathed deeply. She had to get herself under control.

"Hi, Ray." She strove to sound casual. "How are ya?"

"Fine, now that I am with you."

Her pulse jumped, but Ray didn't seem to notice. He continued, "What are you drinking?"

"Ginger ale."

The bartender approached. "What'll it be?"

"I will have the same as my friend. And please bring her another. She is almost finished." Ray smiled at Cami.

She felt unbearably tense, yet expectant. Her skin dampened from nervous excitement. Lifting her hair off her nape to cool down, she wondered, Is this how love feels? Cami hoped not. She didn't know how much more of this she could take. She was about to explode with unexpressed emotions and barely trammeled energy.

Ray moved a warm hand to her knee, below the hem of her dress, which had ridden up onto her thigh. She wasn't wearing panty hose. He squeezed her naked flesh just above the knee.

She couldn't repress a hot quiver of desire. Picking up her glass, she gulped the icy drink, hoping she wouldn't burp out the bubbles. Please, Lord, please let me get through this evening without doing something stupid or embarrassing!

She remembered advice she'd frequently heard, that men loved to talk about themselves. All they needed was a little encouragement. "So, Ray, tell me a little more about yourself. There are...odd rumors around about you."

"Rumors? Of what sort?" His hand fell away from her leg.

She hesitated. She'd probably sound like a fool. "Are you a prince? That seems to be the most popular theory about you."

"Yes, I am what you might call a sheikh."

She almost dropped her soda. A sheikh. A real-live, Arab sheikh here in Texas. Wow. She sought to recover her poise and asked, "What would you call yourself?"

"Rayhan," he said, smiling.

She liked that. He wasn't boastful. "Rayhan. Does your name have a meaning?"

"Yes, it does. It means that I am favored by God." His smile took on an ironic twist, turning into a rueful grimace.

"What's wrong?"

Ray rubbed damp palms on the thighs of his jeans, looking uncomfortable. He paid for the drinks when they arrived before responding. "I am the fourth son and seventh child of my father, who was the ruler of Adnan."

"Isn't that in north Africa, near Morocco?"

"Very good. Most Americans have never heard of Adnan, let alone know its location."

Cami, curious, wanted to discover the source of his obvious unease. "I take it your father didn't think much of fourth sons?"

"No, he did not. My eldest brother is now king. My second brother is his grand vizier. He trained for the position all his life. My third brother runs the military. My sisters married for political advantage."

"And the fourth son?" she asked.

"I have long believed that my chief usefulness is as a spare, ready to be slotted into position should one of my older brothers be harmed or killed." He gave a casual shrug, as if tossing aside his family's rejection.

"That seems unfair." Cami knew her father had spoiled her. She couldn't begin to imagine Ray's feelings when he realized he was disposable rather than valued.

"Life is frequently unfair." The harshness in his voice startled Cami, who hadn't yet seen a rough edge on Ray. Then he shrugged, and she wondered if she'd imagined his anger. He continued, "So I came to America, how would you say it, to make my fortune. There was nothing for me in Adnan. The king refused to consider his worthless fourth son for even a minor position."

Hoping to seem sympathetic, Cami nodded. "I know what you mean. In my father's bedroom he has a photograph of me next to his bed. It's ten years old.

It's hard for me to persuade my father that I'm an adult when he still sees me as a nine-year-old.''

Ray lifted his eyebrows. ''A wonderful insight. Yes. Our parents, and others, stay in the habit of seeing us as we were, not as we are. So I came to America, as you might say, in a huff, determined to prove myself by becoming a success here.''

''And so you raised world-famous, award-winning horses,'' Cami said. ''You showed 'em, all right!''

''Yes, I suppose I did,'' he said, in a wry tone. ''Do you know languages, Cami?''

''Only English and Spanish.''

''Most useful. I wish my English had been better when I came to this country,'' he said.

Cami eyed Ray. She hadn't learned to read his moods, but thought that maybe the conversation bothered him. She could understand why he'd be unhappy over his father's treatment, but languages?

''Did you make your fortune? Are you happy with your life here?'' She hoped he'd say yes, tell her he didn't hide a secret desire to return to his homeland. She wanted to find out what would happen between herself and Ray.

''I have done well, but I believe I may have recently discovered the greatest treasure of all.'' He again caressed her thigh. She tingled from the sheer pleasure of his touch.

He stood and adjusted his jeans. ''Would you like to dance?''

''Yeah, sure would.'' She sipped her soda, then stood.

The band started to play a new tune, and lines began forming for the next dance. Cami was delighted to discover that Ray was as adept on the dance floor as he was on a horse.

And they had fun. When they did the tush push and the bump, Cami found herself turned on by his hips bouncing off hers.

The band started a slow number, and Ray wrapped her in his arms, massaging her bare back above the ruffled edge of her dress. His palm slid; she glowed from his nearness.

Spinning slowly, the mirror ball shed soft shards of red and gold light on his face, reflecting in his deep, brown eyes. Cami's world shrank to contain only Ray, the shimmering lights and the music.

He nibbled on her earlobe. "Delicious," he whispered.

She giggled. "Do you always devour your dates on the dance floor?"

"Only those who taste as sweet as the date palm's fruit." Sliding one hand down to her hip, he drew her closer.

His body pressed, hot and hard, through the layers of clothing separating them. She sucked in an exhilarated breath at his boldness. Her mind whirled.

Releasing her from his embrace, Ray took her hands, squeezing them. "I am going over there." He nodded toward the back of Dancin' Nancy's, where Cami knew a hall led to the rest rooms and an exit. "I will see you at the bar, say, in five minutes?"

Lifting their joined hands to his mouth, he kissed her wrists.

"Okay," she murmured. Returning to the bar, she ordered another soda to cool down. The physical exertion of dancing made her warm, but she knew her sensual heat had another source: Ray.

She'd felt the tension in his body. Though she wasn't experienced, she sensed and understood his male need. But he'd walked away from her before he lost control.

If they continued as they'd begun, there was only one place their relationship would lead: to bed. How should she respond to him? Cami bit her lip.

She had to admit to herself that, in the past, keeping her virginity hadn't been difficult, given that she'd never met anyone who'd tempted her...until Ray.

A tug on her loose hair prompted Cami to swivel her stool around. Jenelle Watson and her husband, Jordy, stood nearby, grinning at her.

"Hey there, Cami!" Jordy hauled her out of the chair and gave her a big, unwanted hug.

Cami pulled loose, peeling him off like duct tape. "Hi Jordy, Jenelle." After hugging Jenelle, Cami surveyed her friend. Though she'd married her high school sweetheart right after their senior class had graduated, Jenelle didn't look happy. Cami looked into her friend's eyes. They held a sadness Cami had never before seen there, despite Jenelle's pregnancy.

Why isn't she happy? Cami wondered. "Hey, let's take a booth." Carrying her soda, she led Jenelle to a quieter spot, away from the speakers. Jordy had already ordered beer. He approached, full glass in hand.

"Jenelle?" He extended the beer to his wife.

Her mouth twisted. "You know the baby and I can't have that."

"How'd you get a beer, anyhow?" Cami asked. "You're underage."

"Money talks, little honey." Jordy winked at her. He returned to the bar.

Little honey? Cami flinched. He'd never called her that. What on earth was going on? Jenelle's lips had gone tight, her jaw tense.

Cami decided to change the subject. "How's the restaurant doing?" Jenelle and Jordy operated a Tex-Mex burger franchise.

"Lousy." Jenelle nodded at Jordy, seated at the bar. "You see how he is. He drinks up all the profits."

"Oh." Cami looked around. Where was Ray?

One of the cowboys came over to their booth and asked her for a dance. She shook her head, preferring to stay with Jenelle and catch up.

Jenelle accepted the cowboy's invitation with a sidelong glance at her husband, still at the bar. Far from resenting her friend, Cami felt sorry for her. Homecoming queen Jenelle had been reduced to dancing with strangers to get attention from her husband. Life hadn't been kind to Jenelle, who was nineteen, pregnant and trapped in a lousy marriage.

The band segued into a slower beat. Cami wished Ray would come back. She missed the tremulous excitement of his embrace. Drawing an excited breath, she remembered his hardness against the softness of her body. She'd burned for him, even through his jeans and her dress. She burned now.

A few moments later, Jordy wandered by and asked Cami to dance. This time, bored from waiting, she agreed.

Within seconds she regretted her decision. An appalling combination of grease, chilis, cigarettes and beer, Jordy's aroma made Cami want to run, not walk, to the nearest door. She guessed he hadn't showered after leaving their burger joint. The green and purple lights flashing across his face added to her queasiness.

Jordy moved closer to whisper in her ear. She couldn't hear what he said since they'd danced close to the speakers. Pulling away from him, she turned her head and yelled, "What?" directly into his ear canal.

He jumped at least a foot.

Cami grinned. That would make him keep his distance. "Sorry."

"I was just saying that you're prettier than ever, Cami Ellison." Jordy glanced at his wife, dancing a few feet away. His gaze dropped to her belly. Disgust flitted across his face.

Cami realized she shouldn't have forced Jordy so far away, so soon. If he'd remained closer, she could "accidentally" step on his feet with her boots. She figured the creep deserved punishment. She didn't like the way Jordy grabbed her to dance, liked his beer breath even less and hated the way he treated Jenelle.

She looked around. Where had Ray gone? "Excuse me," she said to Jordy before walking down the hall toward the rest rooms.

Jordy seized her around the waist and hustled her out the back door.

The night air and harsh outdoor lighting struck her like a blow. She turned, blinking, then wrinkled her nose against the stink of a nearby Dumpster.

Jordy pushed her up against the wall of Dancin' Nancy's. "We ain't done yet, Cami," he said with a crooked smirk. "Don't you remember how you wanted me in high school? Well, now's your chance."

Stunned by his lies, she didn't resist when he shoved his lips onto hers and yanked down her peasant top off her shoulders, tearing it.

Braless, her breasts were exposed to the night air and to his grasp. He grabbed them, twisting one nipple hard and pinching the other as he stuck his tongue into her mouth.

Cami's throat convulsed. Jerking back, she banged her skull painfully against the wall. Dizzy, she dropped her head forward, slamming her forehead against Jordy's nose.

Something warm and wet spurted everywhere. *Blood.* She'd accidentally head-butted his nose. Miraculously, her mind cleared. She stomped on his foot with her cowboy boots as hard as she could, then jerked one knee up sharply, hoping to hit him where it would hurt the most.

Suddenly she was free, her attacker gone, and Ray was there, tossing Jordy against the brick wall. With an "oof" and a yelp, he slid down the side of Dancin' Nancy's in a heap. He curled around himself, mewling and grabbing his genitals.

Now by her side, Ray said anxiously, "Cami? Camille?"

She clutched her head. Her forehead hurt where she'd smashed Jordy's nose. The back of her skull ached at the spot she'd slammed into the wall. Her poor, abused nipples were sore. "I'm all right," she muttered.

"I do not see how." Ray helped her to her feet.

She staggered, leaning into the support he offered. He roped an arm around her, holding her up but not squeezing her hard, as if he understood that a tight grip by a man—any man—right then would have been too much.

Intending to thank him, she looked up at his face. She found his gaze riveted on her naked breasts.

Chapter Three

"Son of a gun!" Cami tried to shove him away. She scrabbled in her pocket for the truck's keys. Damn all men, anyway!

"You should cover yourself up." Ray sounded disapproving.

"What for? You've seen everything." She was overcome with the shock of what had just happened, and what could have happened if she hadn't been able to take Jordy out, or if Ray hadn't shown up. She reeled, close to falling.

Ray caught her, but this time, held her tight. "You've had a bit of a fright, yes? But now it's over." He didn't let her go and continued speaking softly to her. "Cami, you must be more careful."

She rubbed tears out of her eyes with an angry fist. "But I know everyone in McMahon! I grew up here!" She nodded toward Jordy, still limp against the wall. "I've known him since we were kids!"

"People change. Places change." Ray pulled up the tattered top of her dress, concealing her breasts. "A new well opened on the other side of town after you went away to college. There are many oil-field roughnecks and cowboys here you don't know, and who don't know you or your father. There are others who don't care." He jerked a thumb in Jordy's direction.

She sucked in a deep, shuddering breath. "You're right."

He tilted her chin so she'd have to look him in the face. "I want you to stay close to me at night, when you are in McMahon. It is not the same quiet little town you knew when you grew up."

She thought she'd never lose the chill that gripped her insides. "Okay," she whispered. She closed her eyes, letting grief overcome her. When she'd gone to college in San Antonio, she never went anywhere at night without a friend. But she thought she'd be safe back in her hometown. Now she wept for all she'd lost.

"Cami, Cami." Cuddling her close, Ray walked her from Dancin' Nancy's to a small park nearby. In the patch of trees and grass, he sat on a bench, then urged her onto his lap. "Cami, I am so sorry. I should never have left you for so long."

"Wha-what happened? Where were you?"

"Someone wanted to discuss purchasing one of my horses. We went outside to talk. He left a few moments before I saw…" After a sigh laden with regret, he slid his lips across her cheeks, sweeping her tears away.

His tenderness overwhelmed Cami's already shaken defenses. When he touched his lips to hers, she didn't resist, but immediately opened to him. With adrenaline still coursing through her system, but without a threat to overcome, she wanted him more than ever.

She dug her hand into the hair at his nape to bring him in tighter, to make the kiss more intimate. She probed his mouth with her tongue, seeking his male heat and strength. He immediately responded to her, holding her close, his muscles taut. The barely harnessed power in his embrace shook her; she sensed he was under control, but only just.

Ray dragged his mouth away from hers to take several deep breaths. The tension in his body eased. He feathered kisses down her throat and along her collarbone. Clinging to him, her body quivered with need. She tipped back her neck. A small moan escaped her.

The torn edges of cloth at her bodice caressed her tender skin. Ray guided her back onto the bench to nuzzle her cleavage. With a featherlight touch, he smoothed the fabric over her breasts, then caressed her nipples into hard points of want.

She drew in a shivery breath. His gentleness was so at odds with Jordy's roughness that tears again came to her eyes. Without hesitation, Ray circled her taut flesh delicately, as if he knew exactly what she needed. Tiny flashes of pleasure streaked through her. She cried out.

"I want you to be my woman." His voice was low, almost rough.

Dazed, she could only gape speechlessly at him.

"That means no contact with other men. No flirting, no dancing, no kissing."

Still she couldn't find a word to say. She looked into his eyes. The dim light shadowed them into deep pools of desire.

With slow, achingly sensual deliberation, Ray touched one long finger to the hollow of her throat, then drew it down, stroking a line of fiery want to the valley between her breasts, exposed by the torn bodice. He rolled one breast in his palm, then squeezed the very tip of her nipple. He watched her with a narrowed gaze.

Jerking upright, she gasped. Her pulse thundered in her ears. No one, not even the man who'd just mauled her, had ever dared to touch her so. Heat arced to her center.

"Or do you allow any man to handle you in this way?"

The taunting note in his voice galvanized her. She swung her free arm, batting his insolent hands aside. Shocked at her boldness, Cami shrank back into a corner of the bench, tugging her bodice high.

He smiled. "Good. A worthy mate."

"I won't be disrespected." She wiped a trembling wrist across her tingly, sensitive mouth.

Ray leaned back, spreading his arms over the back of the bench in an expansive gesture. "What is the disrespect? I want you. In return I offer myself, absolutely."

Cami stared at Ray. Never had the cultural barrier seemed so wide and deep. What was he talking about?

I want you. I offer myself, absolutely. "Oh!" He wants to be my...my boyfriend? *Boy* wasn't a word she'd apply to Ray. "This is—I didn't think this would happen."

He adjusted his jeans. "No? Never? Have you not used a mirror lately? You're a beautiful woman."

Cami flushed and turned away. She thought she looked about fourteen.

"Listen. We have much to discuss, do we not? Have breakfast with me."

A feminine wariness snaked up her back. Did Ray think she'd spend the night with him?

He smiled slightly. "Only breakfast, nothing more. In town. At Pete's." He jerked his head in the direction of Main Street.

She relaxed. Everyone went to Pete's Diner for his killer breakfasts.

"Ten o'clock tomorrow," he said. "And now I take you home."

"My truck—"

"You should not drive, not after what happened tonight." He lifted her wrist.

Her hand shook.

She curled her fingers into a fist. "I'll be all right. I'll drive real slow."

"I follow you out, yes? Do this for me, Cami. I only wish to keep you safe."

As he drove home, Rayhan watched the red taillights of Cami's truck precede his out of McMahon in the direction of the C-Bar-C Ranch.

Ten years was a long time to harbor a grudge and

plan for revenge. Rayhan hadn't been idle for those years. Far from it. Nor had he remained obsessed with his vengeance. If he had an obsession, it was for his Arabian horses, swift as the wind and beautiful as midnight. After he'd discovered he couldn't drill for oil on his Texas property, he'd turned to his first love: horses. His breeding program, now in its eleventh year, had borne fruit; his Arabians were known throughout the world for their excellence as riding and dressage mounts.

No, he wasn't obsessed, but he was a planner. Honor required him to take revenge upon Charles Ellison, but Rayhan refused to become involved in anything as messy or as inelegant as a lawsuit. Violence was likewise out of the question. In the back of his mind, he'd tucked away the intention that, when she grew up, he'd take Ellison's cherished daughter in exchange for the oil for which he'd paid, but not received. Through her, he'd get what he deserved, and his honor would be vindicated.

Wedding for reasons other than love didn't deter Rayhan. As a royal, he'd always known his wives would benefit him politically or economically. An important undertaking, marriage couldn't depend upon the vagaries of the heart.

He'd occasionally caught sight of Cami as she'd grown, changing from a little ragamuffin into an awkward adolescent. He'd never spoken with her, so he knew nothing of her character.

Now she'd matured into an adult. Instead of viewing her as a simple pawn in his plans, Ray was forced to see Cami for who she was: an intelligent young woman with an excellent mind, determined will and incisive feminine intuition.

He'd wager his finest stallion she'd seen through him when he'd tried to shrug off his father's attitude. The truth was that Rayhan had struggled all his life to prove he was someone who deserved respect, someone other than a useless fourth son.

Impressed by her insight, Rayhan concluded that, depending upon what he did, Cami would become an admirable helpmate through life or a stubborn adversary.

Tonight he'd seen her strength. She'd ably defended herself. Though distressed by the situation, she hadn't panicked.

His heart swelled. She'd be a worthy mother for his children. And as a lover—Ray smiled. He'd learned days ago her kiss was headier than fine cognac. Now he'd tasted of her ardor and her beauty. Her breasts, like peaches, had filled his hands with their heavy sweetness. He'd wanted to take her right then and there, on that park bench in the shadows, but he realized that the waiting would make their eventual coupling all the more wondrous.

Marrying Cami Ellison would accomplish many of his goals. He'd seize the oil wealth he'd wanted for so long while revenging himself on her treacherous father. He'd have a beautiful woman to warm his bed and bear his children. He'd flaunt his wealthy Texan heiress in the faces of his family in Adnan, who'd scorned him all his life.

He clenched his teeth. The last communique from his brother, the king, threatened to affiance Rayhan to a young woman from one of the ever-fractious desert tribes. The king had hinted that Rayhan would be amply rewarded; he surmised the political alliance would force the king to appoint Rayhan to a ministry. Any lesser post would insult the woman's family.

"At last, after so many years, they discover a use for me," he murmured. Bitterness twisted in his belly. Perhaps he'd obey; perhaps he wouldn't.

Could he give up his dreams of a high position in the Adnani government for Cami Ellison and everything she represented?

Cami. Full, soft and fragrant, her breasts had gleamed, pearly in the moonlight. He remembered the taste of her, the feel of her as he'd caressed her nipples. She'd hardened immediately, showing her hidden passion. The mere recollection of that stiff little tip was enough to arouse him.

But his brother claimed Adnan needed Rayhan. Was Cami worth a kingdom?

Cami clutched the steering wheel tightly to avoid bumping all over the rough dirt road to the C-Bar-C. When she approached the gates of home, she pulled into the driveway, then slowed. As she clicked the electric opener, Ray flashed his lights before he continued toward the Double Eagle.

After passing through the gate, she clicked again to close it and drove down the gravel track to the house.

Her relationship with Ray was zipping along at warp speed, and Cami wasn't sure she liked that. She wasn't sure she liked him, either, though she was physically attracted to him in a way she'd never felt.

The way he held and comforted her was beyond anything she'd experienced. She'd wanted to climb inside him, merge with him, become one with him.

But he didn't seem to have listened when she told him she wanted to go slowly. That bothered her.

Tonight he'd asked for a commitment of sorts. *I want you to be my woman.* Becoming his woman would obviously include sex.

Though he offered an equal relationship, he demanded more from her than she was prepared to give. Could she resist his kisses, his touch?

When he'd so gently caressed her hurt breasts, she'd melted. No one had ever touched her there before tonight. She hadn't known a man's comfort could be so good. He'd soothed her pain in a way that, strangely, was more exciting than a lightning storm.

How had Ray known exactly what to do?

Cami drove to her house and parked. Exiting the truck, she closed its door as quietly as she could, to avoid disturbing her father's rest.

She winced at the thought of her father. Cami knew her mom only through photographs. Dad had been both mother and father. He'd given so much to her. He'd run Cami's inheritance—the C-Bar-C—as long as she could remember, even from his hospital bed after a devastating traffic accident. Confined to a wheelchair ever since the accident, he'd lived his life for her.

After she walked to the veranda, she took off her boots before tiptoeing inside her home. Cami guessed her father wouldn't approve of her liaison with Sheikh Rayhan. Aside from the coolness between the Double Eagle and the C-Bar-C, she believed that her father would think Ray too old and too...different for her.

And he'd be right.

Sniffing the familiar aroma of lemon oil, Cami calmed. She decided she'd see Ray at breakfast and serenely inform him she just couldn't accept his flattering offer.

"I'm too young for this," she muttered as she entered the kitchen to search for aspirin and a glass of water.

But later, when she tried to go to sleep, images and remembered sensations haunted her. How good it had been when they'd kissed. Ray's hand on her breast. His approval—his *approval!*—when she'd slapped him. *A worthy mate,* he'd said.

Sounded as though Ray had big plans and she could be the star of his show. Cami rolled onto her back and stared at the ceiling.

Was Ray what she wanted? *Who* she wanted? She only had one virginity and she'd be darned if she'd give it up to just anyone.

But a real-live desert sheikh wasn't just anyone. If he really was a sheikh. But why should that make any difference?

This is the United States of America, and we don't care about royalty, she reminded herself. But if he'd lied—that was bad. She couldn't abide a man who lied to make himself into a big shot.

Cami sighed and gave up on sleep. Clicking on her

bedside light, she got out of bed and went to her desk. Opening her laptop, she pushed the ''on'' button.

After a few minutes of work on the little computer, she found herself staring in amazement at the information she'd discovered on the Internet.

The name of the ruling family of Adnan was ibn-Malik al-Rashad, meaning ''son of the king, the leader.'' Their symbol was the double-headed eagle, symbolizing Adnan's dual nature as a nation of desert tribes and seafarers. Several brothers governed the country, splitting the duties of king, grand vizier, and marshal of the military.

And one of the royal brothers, according to a site she visited, lived quietly in Texas, breeding award-winning riding and dressage horses.

So he's telling the truth. But that shouldn't make any difference, Cami said to herself as she climbed back into bed. Ray was too experienced and too pushy. He wanted more than she could give.

She'd be nice about it, but this romance wasn't going anywhere she didn't choose. Sheikh or not, that was that.

On Sunday morning Pete's Diner bustled. As she entered, Cami could see all the counter stools were full. Waitresses clad in old-fashioned pink polyester uniforms topped by white aprons hustled in and out of the kitchen's swinging metal doors. They carried steaming coffeepots or huge plates heaped with fried foods: eggs, hash brown potatoes, sausage, chicken-fried steaks, biscuits and gravy.

Cami inhaled deeply. The atmosphere, heavy with

the aromas of grease and smoke, smelled like cholesterol heaven. Pete's was a bad place for a diet. Tra-
dition, in the forms of pink polyester, high-calorie
meals and red Naugahyde ruled at Pete's.

Each booth in the row that ran down the street side
of the restaurant was occupied. Several of the patrons
still wore evening clothes. Catching the flash of se-
quins, Cami recognized one of the women who'd gossiped about Ray at Dancin' Nancy's. Lower lids
smeared with last night's eyeliner, the redhead shared
ham and eggs with a cowboy.

Ray sat in the second-to-last booth, chatting with
Billie Mae MacPherson. Dressed in pink polyester,
Billie Mae was leaning over to pour coffee into Ray's
mug while thrusting her D-cups in his face. Or had
they grown to double Ds? Self-conscious, Cami
peeked at her more modest B-cupped pair.

Billie Mae had graduated from McMahon High one
class ahead of Cami. Rumor was that she liked her
cars fast and her men faster. In order to get what she
wanted, had she tinkered with what nature had already so generously given?

Jealousy ignited Cami's innards. Snow would fall
in hot, dusty McMahon before she got beaten out by
Billie Mae, blown-up breasts or not.

Cami stalked down the row of booths, purposely
letting her boot heels clatter on the linoleum floor.
She stopped close enough to Billie Mae to be intim-
idating—or so Cami hoped. Though Billie Mae might
have an admirable bustline, the rest of her develop-
ment hadn't caught up. In boots, Cami stood darn

close to six feet. Billie Mae was barely tall enough to get on the adults' roller coaster at an amusement park.

''Mornin', Billie Mae,'' Cami said, nodding at Ray. ''Hi there, Ray.''

Billie Mae jerked upright and the coffeepot jerked with her. The breasts, however, remained unmoved— a sure sign of medical intervention.

Ray leaped to his feet, dislodging Billie Mae. ''Good morning, Camille.''

Cami sat and so did Ray. Something bumped against her ankle under the table dividing them. She glanced at Ray, whose eyes held that roguish glint she'd learned to welcome. Smiling, he ran his foot up and down her calf. She plucked her T-shirt away from her chest.

''Are you hot, Cami? Billie, please bring a glass of ice water.'' Ray winked at Cami.

''I'd like some coffee, also,'' Cami said.

''Menus?'' Billie asked.

''Sure,'' Ray replied, continuing to play with Cami under the table. Her nipples rose, pushing against her bra. She couldn't believe that he could turn her on by the mere touch of his foot. Billie left and Ray asked Cami, ''How went your sleep?''

''Not so hot.'' After switching off her laptop, she'd tossed restlessly all night.

''I am sorry. Were you unhappy about that fellow who hurt you? We can report him to the police if that is your desire.'' Ray pointed. ''He sits there, with his woman.''

Cami half rose from her seat and twisted her head to see. Ray was correct. Jordy, his nose bandaged, sat with Jenelle at the end of the counter near the door. Cami hadn't noticed them when she'd come into Pete's. She'd seen only Ray.

Neither of her so-called friends had greeted Cami. She wondered what Jordy had told Jenelle. He must have said something, given the big bandage on his nose. Cami gave them a jaunty wave, followed by a tap to her nose and a wink. Jenelle looked puzzled while Jordy glowered.

Shoving them out of her mind, Cami sat back in the padded booth and drew a deep breath. She knew that although she could make light conversation with Ray till the cows came home, she might as well just get to the point.

Her heartbeat increased. She'd spent the entire night aching to hold him tight while sure that a relationship was impossible. ''Jordy wasn't on my mind.'' Cami fiddled with the end of her braid. ''You were.''

''Ah.''

''I'm afraid so.'' She gulped. ''Listen, Ray, we just can't go on like this.''

Chapter Four

Rayhan's chest tightened. His quarry threatened to evade his grasp. "Like what? I was believing that we like each other."

"I like you, but…you're asking me for more than I can give you right now."

Inwardly he cursed his impatience. He wanted her badly, wanted her with all the possessiveness in his soul, wanted to make her his and keep her safe. "I am sorry. You were frightened last night. I tried to comfort you. Did I do wrong?"

"No," she whispered, dropping her gaze to the table. "You were wonderful…too wonderful."

"I do not understand how that can be. You are wonderful to me also. Cami, I hear you when you say you want to go slowly."

She lifted her head. Hope glowed in her lovely blue eyes. "You do?"

"Yes, I do. In Adnan, a man expects his lady to

remain virtuous.'' His gaze slid to Billie Mae, laughing at the counter with one of her customers. The cowboy playfully slapped at her breasts with his Stetson. Rayhan went on, ''I have been with other women in the past, but for you, I stop. All I ask is that we…cleave to each other at this time.''

''I don't understand.''

He sighed. ''I am sorry. Even after so many years, your language is difficult for me. Let me try again. We are getting to know each other. I ask that you not see other men at this time.''

''Oh!'' Pulling a paper napkin from a dispenser, Cami mopped her forehead and nose, looking relieved. ''That's okay. I didn't understand. When you asked me last night to be your woman, I thought—''

''I would be lying if I said I do not want you.'' He surveyed her mouth, her breasts, imagining the sweetness of their eventual coupling. ''But you are not ready.''

''No, I'm not,'' she murmured, looking embarrassed.

He hastened to reassure her. ''That is all right. I wait for you.''

Billie Mae came by with water, coffee for Cami and menus for them both. Cami began to pour vast amounts of virtually every condiment on the table into her mug.

Rayhan peered at her over the rim of his cup, wrinkling his nose. ''I do not understand. Cream, sugar, and what is this? Cinnamon? Why bother to drink the coffee at all?''

She grinned at him. "If they had chocolate, I'd add that, too."

He shuddered. "A waste of fine, fresh coffee."

"Don't people from the Middle East think American coffee is weak?"

"I have grown used to it. In my country, we make the coffee with the grounds in the bottom of the cup. It tastes very different, yes, but it is good. We also drink mint tea." He smiled at her, envisioning Cami, beautifully robed, by his side in the Adnani royal palace. "I would like to take you there someday... someday soon."

"I'd like that. Tell me more about Adnan."

"It is a beautiful country." Ray sat back in his booth and closed his eyes, visualizing the white-washed houses and colorful, mosaic-clad minarets of home. "The word *Adnan* means pleasant, and it is indeed delightful."

"Why did you leave? You obviously love your country very much."

Ray opened his lids. Cami was scrutinizing him with her discomfiting blend of curiosity, intelligence and intuition. He inwardly sighed. One day, probably very soon, he'd have to tell her the truth. This woman was far too smart to deceive.

He wondered how long it would take her to discover his true motives for their relationship. He wanted her, yes, but still...

"As I explained, there was nothing for me to do there. After I finished university, I wanted a post, but my father, who was king at that time, refused to listen. I held out some hope after my brother ascended to

the throne, but…'' He gave a fatalistic gesture. ''The
new king was accustomed to seeing me as his useless
younger brother. Nothing could persuade him to give
me the responsibilities I believe I deserve.''

Billie Mae returned to take their orders. Cami ordered cereal and fruit with skim milk. Rayhan asked
for a sausage omelette.

''You eat pork?'' she asked.

''Yes. I am, how can I say it, a fallen Muslim. I
do not believe in very much, Cami.''

''Do you believe in God or Allah?''

He shrugged. ''I believe I am not in a position to
say what, or who, dwells in the heavens.''

''Do you believe in…love?''

Rayhan looked into her eyes. Sweetly romantic, her
gaze reminded him of summer evenings, the scent of
jasmine and stolen kisses. ''When I am with you, I
believe in love.''

Cheeks growing pink, Cami dropped her gaze to
the table, rubbing her thumb along its cracked, uneven
edge. He noticed she'd cut her nails short, but buffed
them until they were shiny. Good. He didn't like the
painted claws on some women. They looked predatory, like lizards or hawks.

He'd been with many females, but none with
Cami's intriguing personality. She could, by turns, be
modest and passionate, innocent and intelligent, in-
sightful and naive.

She was really quite fascinating.

Their meals arrived and Rayhan dug into his with
an appetite. He was hungry. He'd awakened early and
ridden along the boundary of their adjoining proper-

ties, hoping to catch a glimpse of Cami. He'd known it was foolish, because he'd be seeing her later, but he enjoyed her and had wanted to see her as soon as possible. He told himself that the more they met, the more quickly his revenge would come to fruition.

Cami tore open a box of cornflakes and emptied them into a bowl. She picked up a banana, peeled it halfway down, and sliced it on top of her cereal. Then she poured milk over everything.

"Would you like some of my eggs? There are plenty." Rayhan waved a forkful of his omelette in front of Cami's face. Her eyes tracked it like radar. He grinned.

"N-no, thank you." She crunched a mouthful of cornflakes. "Aren't you worried about cholesterol and fat?"

"You are shy about your appearance. Why is that? You are so lovely." He thrust the eggs into his mouth, chewed and swallowed.

Cami scowled. "I have a tummy and fat thighs."

"What is it about American women? All of you are obsessed with skinny. Do you want to look like this fork?"

"No, but—"

"Of course you have a tummy. Where else would you put your food? Your thighs are not fat."

"Are so." She ate more cereal.

"Are not. I felt them last night, remember?" He grinned at the memory. He'd dreamed about lying between her splendid thighs. "I am in a position to say whether or not they are fat. They are not fat." He offered her a bite of eggs.

She blushed again, most attractively. "I'm glad you think they're okay."

"They are not only okay. They are perfect." So perfect he wanted to run his tongue over every glorious inch.

"But letting you feed me is…" She faltered, as though she lacked the right words to express herself.

"Intimate." Rayhan knew that the sharing of their meals would link them in a subtle but definite way. "But they're just eggs, Cami, not an engagement ring."

Her mouth popped open. "A ring?"

In went the eggs. She was so delightfully transparent that he couldn't stop a victorious smirk from crossing his face. He carefully withdrew the fork from her mouth before eating the last bite on his plate. "Finish your cereal. Are you going to eat the rest of that banana?" Rayhan left his side of the table to scoot beside her on the bench seat.

"I might."

He settled his hand on Cami's vulnerable nape, knowing his intimate touch was a public declaration of their relationship. She cuddled closer, easing her long, curvy body into his side. Caressing her neck, he ran the tips of his fingers up and down its length, then slid his hand down her neck to stroke her bare arm.

Cami purred, catlike. The sensuous murmur pleasantly tickled his nerve endings. Heat radiated throughout his body.

He picked up the banana with his free hand and set the peeled portion to her lips.

She drew in a breath, then opened her mouth. He smiled.

* * *

Ashamed that she'd neglected her father, Cami headed straight for their shared office upon her return to the C-Bar-C. Since she'd turned thirteen, she and her father had spent four hours every afternoon on the accounts, with few days free. The only breaks occurred when she attended college. Now, because she'd returned, they picked up where they'd left off, adding additional management responsibilities to the list of tasks Cami regularly completed.

Cami had always been aware that the Crowell oil belonged to her, though the livestock was the Ellisons'. The distribution of the ranch's assets didn't make any difference to her. She knew she'd be a wealthy woman because she'd inherit both fortunes one day. And when she graduated from college, she'd manage her holdings, leaving her father free to retire if he chose.

"Ready for work, Dad?"

Seated in his wheelchair behind his massive, dark oak desk, her father folded the sports section with a rustle. One graying, bushy eyebrow arched as Charles quizzically regarded her. "What's up, kiddo?"

Cami sighed. She should have known she couldn't hide her chaotic emotions from her father. She never could fool anyone, not even when she played a donkey in the Christmas pageant and wore a big fake head with a long nose and ears. Everyone somehow knew it was her.

Unfortunately, she didn't know how to respond to his question. She was feeling too many emotions, all at once. Edgy with nervous energy. Excited that she had a hottie in her life. Scared her father wouldn't approve of Ray. Heck, *she* didn't even approve of her romance with Ray.

An honest person, she didn't like to evade, but this time she did. She figured Charles really wouldn't want to know if she started an intimate relationship with a man. That would just worry him, wouldn't it?

Cami searched for the right words. Her father hadn't been healthy since a traffic collision shattered his hip and his pelvis, causing numerous internal injuries, some of which had never healed right. He'd never walk again unaided, and only occasionally could use a cane to get around. Cami didn't want to say anything that would make his condition worse.

She cleared her throat. "I'm just…edgy. I guess I need to get out more. Though I went dancing last night and then had breakfast at Pete's with some friends." Darned close to the truth.

"Great!" Her father's approval made her stomach twist with guilt. "I'm glad you're stepping out. You don't need to stay home with your old dad, watching reruns and videos."

"Oh, Daddy." Cami stooped to hug her father around his shoulders. Pitifully thin, they frightened her. "I don't mean to imply I'm bored with you."

"I know you're not, darlin'." Her father paused to take a hit from his inhaler, which he kept in his top desk drawer. Charles, who also suffered from asthma, spent most of his time indoors during the summer, avoiding pollen and dust. "It's natural that at your age you want a little excitement."

"I had a little too much excitement last night." Cami gave her father a censored version of her encounter with Jordy, saying only that he'd made a heavy pass at her. Details weren't necessary and would upset her father. She finished, "I don't know what I should do. I hate to think of him cheating on Jenelle and drinking up all the money she'll need for the baby."

"I can probably take care of Jordy's drinking in McMahon with a word or two in the right ears."

"Really?" Cami slipped behind her smaller desk and flipped on switches to start her computer.

"Sure. He's underage, isn't he?" Charles reached for his Rolodex. "So, have you met a fella?"

Cami jumped a foot. So much for keeping Dad in the dark. "Uh, yeah. I—"

Her father held up a hand. "Don't tell me anything more unless you want to, Cami. I trust you to make appropriate decisions."

"But I'm not sure about him, Dad."

"What's the problem?"

"He's a lot older." There. She'd done it. She'd told her father the truth.

Her father frowned. "Is he married?"

"Oh, no!" A swell of relief lightened her. "In fact, he told me he doesn't want to see anyone else while we're dating. And he doesn't want me to, either."

Charles looked thoughtful. "That makes sense. Otherwise, how can you really trust each other?"

* * *

Her father's support buoyed her spirits, but Cami couldn't entirely excuse her conduct. She hadn't told Charles everything. On the other hand, he hadn't wanted the particulars.

Worse, Ray hadn't made a date with her after they'd finished breakfast at Pete's. He'd paid the tab, politely escorted her to her truck, then treated her to a goodbye kiss that would have curled her hair had it not been in a braid.

But he hadn't asked to see her again. Cami fretted. She didn't know what to do. Normally, with any other friend, she'd simply phone or e-mail. But Ray wasn't just anyone. He was older, and from a traditional culture. She didn't think he liked forward women. He'd made it clear that he preferred modesty, saying, "In Adnan, a man expects his lady to remain virtuous."

She wanted to be Ray's, but didn't know if she could give up the freedoms that came with being a modern American girl.

Maybe she could have it all. Cami brightened at the thought. Ray had never said anything about living in Adnan, merely visiting. Surely he wouldn't expect her to live anywhere but her beloved C-Bar-C. And if they stayed in Texas, she'd have it all: her desert prince and her home.

They hadn't planned another meeting, but Rayhan nevertheless felt serene about the situation. He didn't want to pressure Cami, so he'd decided to wait until the bird came to hand of her own will.

He made himself available, frequently riding along the shared edge of their properties at dawn and dusk.

Sundown came later in June, so often his evening ride took place close to nine at night. He enjoyed the long days; they reminded him of home.

But tonight's sunset, with its humidity and dust, its scent of horses and cottonwoods, was distinctly Texan. Tired after a long day spent training a filly to bridle, Rayhan allowed Kalil to wander as the gelding chose. Kalil picked a familiar path, the one that led to the swimming hole near the C-Bar-C.

Fed by an underground spring, its waters remained fresh throughout even the hottest summers, feeding lush greenery that protected it from the stares of passers-by. At this late hour, the hands who worked his spread were relaxing in the bunkhouse or had gone to town to have some fun. Only Rayhan, impelled by a restlessness he didn't understand, still roamed the Double Eagle.

Bands of pink and coral streaked the darkening sky. In a few minutes the heavens would transmute into a magical shade of blue that always reminded Rayhan of Cami's eyes.

Would he encounter her this evening? His pulse quickened at the thought.

Kalil poked his nose through the greenery surrounding the swimming hole and chuffed.

Rayhan, hearing a splash, dismounted to check the source of the sound.

Ah. Cami. He surmised she'd been riding hard, because Sugar stood hock-high in the water…and Cami was entirely submerged, but for her blond head. Then she rolled so she floated on the surface of the pond. Even in the dimming light, he could see the tops of her breasts above the water. Though covered with some flimsy fabric, they swayed with the slight current.

Rayhan walked toward the water's edge.

Cami rose, standing thigh deep in the pond. The glowing sunset's light shimmered off the water sliding down the curves and planes of her body. She looked like a naiad emerging from an enchanted pool.

He couldn't speak, couldn't breathe, couldn't even think.

Even in the waning light, he could see she wore only a tiny pair of panties and a thin, cropped top. His gaze traveled down her tapering rib cage to her narrow waist. Crystalline drops nestled in her navel, inviting his tongue. Her torso flared to lovely, rounded hips and a wide pelvis, designed to carry a child.

His child. Rayhan drew a shuddering breath.

Her wet, pink panties couldn't conceal much, but the dimming light hid her secrets.

He stepped forward, deliberately crunching a branch underfoot to attract her attention. He wanted to give her the opportunity to come to him.

Chapter Five

Cami's skin chilled. Who was there?

She scanned the bank of the pond, seeing nothing in the shadows. A night bird flapped its wings, startling her.

A branch cracked. Then a dark shape emerged from the shrubbery.

Dressed in swirling robes, he appeared a wild creature born of myth and legend. He seemed not to walk but to flow gracefully as he approached the riverbank, a fey spirit of the night.

Impelled by an instinct she couldn't control, Cami went to meet him at the water's edge. She was acutely aware of everything around her: the squish of mud beneath her bare feet; the buzzing of insects; the evening scents of the foliage; her heartbeat, which had leaped to a frantic pace when she saw who stood by the stream.

Ray awaited her with the posture of a sultan who'd summoned his houri.

Yet he hadn't said a word. He didn't need to. Strong and tall, infinitely compelling and mysterious, he lured her to him without effort, the way man had drawn woman to his side since the dawn of history.

She couldn't see his expression in the dusk. Nervous, she guessed he'd dislike her spontaneous decision to strip to her undies and swim. Maybe this conduct wasn't what an Adnani male expected from a virtuous woman.

Now she stood before him. Her heart raced.

He reached forward to cup one breast in his palm. With dark, tapered fingers, he flicked her nipple through the damp silk of her camisole.

It puckered into a taut, needy point. She closed her eyes, focusing on the blissful ache. Her knees shook, and she concentrated on staying upright.

"Watch," he said, his voice soft with amazement. "See how your breast trembles in my hand."

Shy, Cami turned her face away.

He laughed.

Starch stiffened her spine, and she cut him a glare. How dare he laugh at her?

"Cami." But he didn't mock. Instead, he seduced. He bent her back over his arm to kiss her nipples, arousing first one, then the other. Excitement flared; she felt the tender flesh crinkle and tighten against the pressure of his tongue and teeth. Sucking in a breath, she pushed her breast into his mouth, chasing the pleasure.

He slipped his hand between her unresisting thighs, stoking the fire with clever, knowledgeable fingers.

Cami's moist, ready mouth, heavy-lidded eyes, her sweet gasps and pants told Rayhan she was ready for his love. Draped over his arm she lay, vibrating with need, offering herself to him, a sensual banquet.

He'd feast on her soon, but not tonight. He caressed her one last time. She writhed in his arms, his for the taking. Rather than have her on the riverbank, he set her on her feet, smoothing away tousled strands of hair from her flushed face.

She reached for him, tugging on his robes to draw him closer, molding her curves against his hardness beneath the loose folds of his *thobe*. His body jerked; he fought to master his urge to possess her immediately. When she tried to pull away he didn't let her go, palming her bottom to push her intimately against him.

"Did you think I remained unmoved?" He let his voice growl in her ear. Holding her close, he eased her along the evidence of his passion. He flicked his tongue over her quivering mouth, first testing the tender inner surface of her lip, where the flesh was so sensitive, then entering her deeper, in and out.

He licked the dainty whorl of her ear, then blew upon it.

She shivered, sinking into his embrace, as though she sought his warmth. He wrapped her in his arms, enfolding her in his robes.

With Ray Cami felt utterly safe, swathed in his silky cocoon. But his demanding kisses and virile body reminded her of the threat he posed. The tension in his limbs signaled her that he was frighteningly close to losing control. If he succumbed to his instincts, she couldn't protect her innocence from him. He was too strong, too seductive, and too tempting.

"Soon," he purred in her ear.

She tugged away.

"Soon. Cami, I know how to treat a woman. I promise. I will show you." He put a finger to his chin, looking thoughtful.

"Show me…how?"

His smile made her every cell tingle with delighted anticipation, even though she knew nothing would happen. It couldn't.

"Come to the Double Eagle. Alone. In, hmm, three days, at sundown."

"Sundown?"

"Yes. The meeting of light and dark. Male and female." He touched her breast, again plucking the nipple into aching desire.

Lightning streaked through her body.

"Come to me."

Come to me. Ray had the most compelling way of making a simple dinner date sound like an invitation to adventure. As the sun set three days later, Cami turned the key to start one of the C-Bar-C's trucks, wondering how he did it.

It was the sheikh thing. Shoving her foot on the accelerator, she shook her head with exasperation. She fell for his line over and over again. How could she be such a sap?

I know how to treat a woman. Not that she'd find

out tonight. She'd protected herself from the possible outcome of the evening as best she could without breaking the date. No makeup; maybe he wouldn't think her attractive. But except for their date at Dancin' Nancy's and some goop over her zit, she hadn't worn cosmetics any time she'd seen Ray. He didn't seem to notice the difference. So much for facials and manicures.

Panty hose, even though Cami hated them, especially in midsummer. But any garment that encased her from waist to heels was a good idea. She would have donned a chastity belt if one existed in Texas, but had settled for an underwired bra and unsexy, brief-style panties.

Atop the restricting hose, she wore a calf-length, crinkled silk skirt, with a loose tunic top that made her look five months pregnant.

With any luck she'd have a pleasant evening, a good meal and then leave without getting in too deep with Ray Malik—or, rather, Prince Rayhan ibn-Malik al-Rashad.

With a gusty sigh she acknowledged to herself it was probably too late. She'd fallen for him faster than Juliet for Romeo. Cami just hoped her romance would turn out better.

She turned out of the C-Bar-C toward the Double Eagle. Her fingers shook slightly as they clasped the steering wheel, so she clenched them tighter, grumbling in annoyance under her breath. She was *such* a ninny.

But she couldn't stop the whirling excitement in her heart, which seemed to engender a sensual heat that spread, unwelcome and unstoppable, deep into her belly. She squirmed on the seat, feeling as though her frame, though tall, still wasn't big enough to contain her roiling emotions.

Bursting at the seams with pure sexual energy, she twitched with a restless coiling need she instinctively knew could be slaked in only one way—by taking the man she desperately wanted into her body.

She approached the Double Eagle, slowing the truck, then stopping next to a small white gatehouse at the ranch entrance. The guy inside the tiny wooden structure wore a *gutra* headdress, like Ray's. He waved her on.

Cami looked around as she drove through Ray's spread. Despite the dimming light, she could discern orderly corrals, stock, even crops. Alfalfa, she guessed, for the horses. No oil derricks or pumps, though. She wondered why. She knew a huge pool of oil lay beneath McMahon. Her land was rich with oil; wasn't his?

She shunted aside those mundane thoughts when she neared Ray's home, a big house on a rise about a half mile away from the gate. She guessed he'd built it himself. What other Texas ranch house flaunted a minaret?

She stopped at the entrance, marked by an elaborate wrought iron gate. From the outside, the house looked like an intriguing mixture of Spanish and Arab styles, with whitewashed walls and an orange tiled roof. Windows were covered with charming grillwork, seeming more decorative than designed for defense.

Though, as a sheikh, he'd be security conscious, wouldn't he? But the beautiful rose vines lacing the wrought iron belied any safety concerns.

Ray awaited her at the arched front entrance. Dressed tonight in white, flowing robes, he looked cool and comfortable as he opened her door and helped her alight.

Not so Cami. When she left the air-conditioned truck, she found the panty hose stifled her. She felt like fried sausage stuffed into a too-tight casing.

"Cami." He kissed her forehead and took her hand. She noticed he had calluses on his palms and fingers from training his Arabians, in the same spots she'd grown the tough, hard skin working with her horse.

He led her up broad, tiled steps into his home.

Ray's home.

He didn't have a front door. An elaborate wrought iron gate protected an archway, clad with mosaics. After she passed, the gate clanged shut behind her, signaling her entrance into his domain. Her pulse beat unsteadily in her ears.

She fiddled with the end of her braid. He guided her with an arm around her shoulders through a tiled walkway, sublimely cool, toward an area filled with glowing turquoise light.

Suddenly the hall opened into an enormous courtyard lined with plants and—oh, merciful heavens—the most gorgeous swimming pool she'd ever seen, glimmering in the dusk like a giant aquamarine lozenge.

Her panty hose, already uncomfortable, abruptly

became unbearable. She wanted to tear them off and run screaming like a kid into that lovely water. Sweat broke out on her upper lip.

"You look hot, Cami." Ray surveyed her with obvious concern. "Would you like a swim? The water is very nice. I keep it cool but not cold."

Looking into his eyes, Cami couldn't detect a trace of guile.

"I promise, you will remain unmolested. None of my servants would dare to touch a guest of mine." He spoke with the unconscious arrogance of a prince accustomed to total obedience.

He'd probably have anyone who dared to hassle his female guests shot at dawn. But it was Ray Cami feared. Ray, and her reaction to him. Taking off her clothes and swimming in his pool—no. No. She might as well jump into his bed.

But she couldn't bring herself to refuse. Her lips simply wouldn't form the words *No, thank you.*

"Come." He again took her by the arm and led her down the length of the courtyard, along the right side of the pool. Open to the sky, it didn't smell of chlorine but of the roses and dwarf citrus that lined his home's whitewashed walls.

A fountain splashed into the pool. Her boots clattered while Ray, barefoot, made no sound. He stopped short of the end of the courtyard before a pair of French doors. Opening them, he ushered her into a room with a bed, a dresser and closets. Though it appeared comfortable, its unused air showed Cami it was a guest room. An opulent, patterned spread covered the bed. Carpets softened the tiled floors underfoot.

Ray went to a closet to remove a white toweling robe. "Swim in your bra and panties if you wish." His rogue's smile returned. "But I would not mind if you shed all your clothes. Meanwhile, I will get you some juice to drink. Cami, you are overheated."

His nose crinkled with disapproval. She tried not to chuckle, but he was so darn cute when he did that.

He continued, "You should not let yourself become dehydrated in this weather." He disappeared, closing the French doors behind him.

Cami swallowed against her sticky throat. He was right. The enveloping clothes she'd selected, plus her boots, had been stupid choices for the triple-digit weather and high humidity of the day. Though close to dusk, the air still held an unhealthy sultriness.

She stripped down to her lingerie and noted in the mirror that her prudish underclothing hid her body more effectively than most bikinis. Picking up the robe, she donned it before leaving the cool, cave-like darkness of the guest room for the courtyard. She dropped the robe onto one of two chairs set next to a nearby table, then dived into the pool.

It was heaven on earth. The C-bar-C didn't have a swimming pool, so she occasionally swam in the creek. Fastidious, she never dipped in her head and always showered after; animals occasionally used the pool as a watering hole. She loved to swim, but hadn't used a chlorinated pool since she left college.

Rayhan entered, bearing a tray with a pitcher, a bucket of ice and two glasses. He set it on the table near Cami's robe. Sitting, he watched her splash and play. Though tempted to join her, he decided to maintain a respectful distance. He'd promised her she wouldn't be pestered.

He'd keep that promise even if he exploded with want.

Rayhan's body had gone into alert upon taking Cami's arm to escort her out of her truck. The clothes she'd selected—a colorful skirt, modestly long, with a matching shirt—suggested rather than revealed her charms, piquing his interest. Then he noticed how overheated she'd become. "Foolish child!" he muttered to himself.

When they married, he vowed to himself, he'd take good care of her. No more seminude swimming in unsanitary ponds visited by horses and cowboys. No gallivanting around in midsummer, courting heat stroke.

He hoped his nemesis, Charles Ellison, would appreciate everything Rayhan would do for Cami. Despite himself, he felt a flash of sympathy for the man. Rayhan was aware of Ellison's incapacity. Managing a willful teenager on top of severe injuries couldn't have been easy.

If all went according to plan, Ellison would be responsible for his daughter no more. Her husband would manage Cami's life—and her fortune.

The pool quieted. Rayhan glanced over to see Cami floating on her back, her bra-encased breasts thrusting above the water. Her nipples had wrinkled, and the sharp tips poked the cups, showing pink through the wet, sheer fabric.

Rayhan leaned back in his chair, enjoying the show. Grateful for his loose, concealing *thobe,* he realized tight jeans would be agony.

But this flirtation had to stop before he burst from frustration. Woman existed to satisfy man, he told himself. And Cami Ellison existed to satisfy him, whether she knew it or not. He had to convince her they belonged together.

In the meantime they both needed to cool down.

Hard, chilly pellets dropped from the sky onto Cami's unprotected belly. She opened her eyes to see Ray standing poolside, tossing ice cubes at her.

"Hey!" Cami ducked under the water, then came up by the side of the pool. She splashed Ray, nailing him solidly in the midsection. The water rendered his white robes translucent from waist to knees, sticking the fabric to his body.

She gasped. She couldn't look away from that fascinating shadowy area at Ray's pelvis.

His laughter jolted her out of her examination. He plopped onto a deck chair and howled, clutching his side.

Completely mortified, Cami ducked under the water, hoping he'd leave to change before she emerged.

No such luck. Instead, he sat at the side of the pool, dangling his legs into the water, still laughing at her.

She didn't understand. "I thought you liked modest women."

"I like *you.* Come." He held out a hand to her.

She took it and let him tug her out of the pool. He

handed her the toweling robe, still chuckling, then poured a drink for her.

Cami rubbed the folds of the robe over her face and body, then put it on, tying its cord around her waist. She took the glass and sipped, savoring the sweet, cold orange juice. "It's yummy. From your trees?" She nodded at the dark, glossy citrus trees lining the courtyard.

Ray visibly swelled with pride. "I squeezed it myself, just for you."

Hmm. She tipped her head to one side, seeing him in a new light. "You like to do things for yourself, don't you?"

He looked jolted. "What? Princes do not do… things. We are worthless creatures. Especially fourth sons." He gave her a little, puzzled frown.

Cami shook her head, remembering the calluses on his palms and fingers. "Not you. You don't have to, but you squeeze your own orange juice and train horses. You like to use your hands to accomplish goals, make things happen."

"Your insights are always surprising. Perhaps you are right." Ray shrugged. "I greatly enjoy this ranch. Of course, my Arabians are my pride. I especially love to watch the breeding mares, and dream about their foals. Whether they will be male or female, gray, dun or black, sharp tempered or easy."

This man will make an excellent father. The thought swept through Cami's mind like a tornado. She stared at Ray, noting every detail anew: wide, intelligent eyes; his hands, precise and elegant as he poured himself juice; his sensitive mouth. She quivered when she remembered how his lips felt on hers.

She evaluated the components not merely as a lover, but the way a single woman views an unattached male...as a prospective partner through life.

Then she recalled that Ray had brought up marriage at their first meeting. He'd told her she'd be a worthy mate the night outside Dancin' Nancy's. He'd mentioned a ring the next morning, at Pete's.

On top of it all, he'd admitted noticing her before they'd met. She'd dismissed all those statements at the time as flirtation, figuring he just wanted to get into her pants.

Cami sucked in a breath.

What if he were for real?

At this point, nothing about the way Ray operated would surprise her. From a different culture, she'd learned he couldn't be judged by American standards.

She eyed him. Despite his royal birth, here was a man willing to dirty his hands raising horses and even squeezing fruit for his girlfriend.

Ray topped off her juice. "Drink."

Cami examined Ray over the rim of her glass. A nurturer. That was it. Ray was a nurturer. Plus, he was so sexy she couldn't keep her hands off him. She wanted to climb inside his skin and merge with him.

One of the women's magazines she'd read advised that to get a man, a woman had to know what she wanted. She had to list desirable traits.

Cami had never bothered. At her age she'd never considered marriage.

But now she stared at Ray and tried to order her

scrambled thoughts. She didn't need a man to take care of her financially or protect her physically; she knew she could handle herself.

So what did she need?

She needed a nurturer. She needed someone who'd be a good father for their children.

That was it. She set the empty glass onto the table with a decisive clatter. If he asked, she'd say yes, and to heck with the age difference.

Chapter Six

Cami stopped her speculations short. Was she nuts? Talk about counting chickens before they hatched! Ray hadn't asked her to marry. He'd never met her father. And how long had they known each other— maybe ten days?

She needed space. "I'd like to get dressed now." She retreated to the guest room.

"There's a shower in that suite," Ray said. "You may rinse your hair if you wish."

Fifteen minutes later Cami was ready to rejoin Ray in the courtyard, barefoot, with only her long skirt and loose top covering her nudity. Her skin shivered with sensual electricity. As she moved, her breasts swayed, the nipples brushing the rough gauze fabric of her tunic.

She peeked through the French doors. The glass-topped table, now set for two, was flanked by matching, wrought iron chairs, their backs and seats padded with patterned cushions. Mellow light from enameled brass candlesticks softened the planes of Ray's face.

Absorbed, he bent over a platter, fussing with the garnish around a golden-crusted pie.

When she stepped into the courtyard, he looked up. He smiled and left his task. "Cami." Now by her side, he took her hand to kiss the palm. The tiny hairs on her arm shifted in response to his touch. Ray led her to the table where he poured a pale golden wine into two glasses.

"I don't know if I should drink," Cami said.

"I won't permit you to indulge to excess. Drunkenness is a most unflattering condition. Here is water for you, also." He lifted his glass. "To love."

Cami sipped, conscious of his intense scrutiny. Though she'd dated, she'd never been wooed, courted, *pursued* with such blatant hunger. She sensed his urgency and thought she understood its source. Men had needs. No doubt he'd try to bed her tonight. She'd tell him no, once again. She had to.

She might be old-fashioned, but she knew she'd fallen in love with this beautiful, complicated man, fallen for his Arab prince mystique and his sheer maleness.

He had a complex inner life and a mysterious past she didn't yet understand, she mused, but she'd love to unravel the intricate tapestry of everything that was Ray, even if the task took a lifetime. His secrets cloaked him with an air of mystery and intrigue, compelling her the same way hidden treasure baited a pirate.

She had to have him in her life. But if they made

love without marriage, he could easily move on, she reasoned. He'd be more likely to stick around after lovemaking if she had his ring on her finger.

If he dumped her, she didn't know if she'd ever be able to love again. Though marriage couldn't ensure happiness, she figured they had a better chance if they wed.

Cami set down her glass, remembering that when people got drunk, they got stupid.

"Let us eat."

Ray picked up a knife and sliced into the pie, releasing a cloud of aromatic steam scented with cinnamon.

Cami sniffed appreciatively. "What's that?"

"I have for you a simple meal tonight. Tabouleh salad and b'stila, a pigeon pie with almonds, egg and raisins."

"Did you cook?"

"But yes. The servants have the night off. I wished to be undisturbed."

"You cooked?" Cami couldn't get over it. Ray, a prince, had squeezed her orange juice, baked her b'stila and tossed her tabouleh salad.

He placed a wedge of pie on a blue earthenware plate, then heaped tabouleh next to it. Then he artistically arranged flat-leaved parsley nearby. He smiled at her. "Yes, I cook."

"You are not a useless fourth son."

"No, I am not. Since I came to Texas ten years ago, I have worked hard to—how would you say it— overcome the accident of my birth and make a life for myself.'' He served himself tabouleh and b'stila. ''Eat.''

Cami ate and drank. The food was delicious, almost good enough to overcome her excitement at Ray's presence by her side. And he couldn't seem to keep his hands off her. He scooted his chair close to hers, fed her choice bits of pigeon from his plate, interspersed with kisses, and plied her with wine until she pushed his hand away.

''Enough,'' she said. ''Or I'll suspect you of getting me drunk so you can have your way with me.''

''You would suspect correctly. One night I hope to get lucky with you.''

''In your dreams.'' Cami waved her water glass in the air, feeling cheerfully loose and relaxed.

''Yes, you are, every night. But I will not push. You, Cami, must come to me of your own free will.''

''Dream on.''

''I know you wouldn't have just anyone, but am I still just anyone?'' His eyes went wide and pleading.

''Sorry, prince.'' Cami balanced her last bite of b'stila on her fork. ''I'm saving myself for marriage.''

''Marriage! You set a high price on your love. But perhaps you are right to do so.'' Ray laughed softly, leaning into his chair. He angled his head back. ''Look there.'' He pointed into the moonless sky. ''Mars.''

''How can you tell?''

She chewed and swallowed the last delicious bite.

''It is slightly red. Let me show you.''

Taking her hand, he led her to a wooden door at the base of the minaret.

As they climbed the twisting, turning stairs, Cami felt as though she'd left Texas to ascend into a new, magical world, where mysteries would be revealed and secrets discovered. Her breath shortened, and her heart tripped as she trod the long spiral stair up the narrow tower.

It was dark, the only illumination starlight filtering through occasional slits in the minaret's walls. She couldn't see much. Her senses constricted to encompass only their harsh inhalations, the coolness of the tiled stairs beneath her bare feet and the warmth of Ray's hand on her waist, which sent tremors of longing through her.

Finally the staircase ended, opening into a large circular room at the very top of the minaret.

Eight arched apertures, unglassed and open to the night, rimmed the octagonal room. Through them, Cami could hear the twitter of birds and an occasional bark from a dog as the Double Eagle's animals settled down for the night.

The only furniture in the room was a neat desk, two stools and a large structure covered with a plastic tarp. Releasing her hand, Ray twitched aside the tarp to reveal a telescope.

''I sit up here many a night, star-watching.'' His voice had gone soft and a little hesitant, she thought, as if he revealed a secret, precious place within himself.

''Wow,'' she breathed, circling the room so she could investigate everything.

''Now, let me prove to you that Mars is truly the

red planet.'' Ray expertly twirled dials, adjusting the complex scope.

He showed her Mars, and Saturn, with its fabulous rings, then explored with her deeper into the universe. Cami saw Sirius, blazing blue-white in the night, and a double star, its two halves improbable shades of turquoise and gold, flashing in the heavens, locked together by gravity in an infinite dance.

''The colors are amazing.'' Cami looked at Rayhan with a bedazzled gaze.

''They're no more lovely than your eyes.'' He took both her hands in his. ''Cami, I brought you here to show you my heart, the deepest part of myself. I want you to have, to know, all of me.''

At the penultimate moment, doubts assailed Rayhan. What if he was moving too fast for Cami? He sensed she wanted him, yes, but she was a modern, independent woman with a strong will for one so young. She'd rarely mentioned marriage as part of her plans. What if she—

His hand closed around the box in a pocket of his *thobe*. He fingered its rounded edges and corners, taking comfort in its solidity. Don't borrow trouble, he told himself. Rayhan remembered how he'd felt at age nineteen, how desire tore at his body and mind until he'd have done anything to quench his lust.

Cami was a healthy young female. He'd caught her poised on the cusp of womanhood and deliberately awakened her sensuality in gradual stages. They'd come close the other evening at the creek; he was sure he could have brought her to fulfillment, but instead he'd stopped the seduction short. He'd intended to drive her wild, then leave her empty and needy.

He wanted all of her, not merely her body, but her heart and her soul. Nothing would satisfy him but a complete conquest.

Rayhan inhaled, letting his breathing calm. He pulled out the box.

He swallowed. "For you," he whispered. "And with it, my heart."

Cami reached for the box, her fingers quivering. She opened it. Inside, tucked into a fold of white satin, twinkled a heart-shaped diamond set in a platinum band.

She dropped the box. It disappeared into the dark shadows of the room.

"Oh, I'm so sorry!" Looking distressed, she put a hand to her mouth before peering at the floor. "It must have landed with the white side down. Will we ever find it?"

"Of course." Despite his tension and exasperation, Rayhan struggled to stay calm. Kneeling at her feet, he swept the tile with an open palm, quickly locating the box. "I did not know my proposal would so alarm you."

"I'm not alarmed, just a little surprised. I'd thought about it, and wondered if you had also. Is it for the sex?"

Her candor startled him. Though chaste, Cami's ability to discuss sex openly was uncharacteristic of women he'd known. They either evaded or flirted. Not so Cami. Her honesty about everything was her trademark. Wishing to respond as truthfully, he hesitated. Should he reveal his long-held plans? She would surely believe his calculated seduction and hidden motives deceitful.

"Well, I listened when you said you wanted to take it slow, but I do want to have you. I cannot lie about that."

She boldly touched him through his *thobe*. His body reacted to the first brush of her questing hand. "No, you sure can't," she said with a smile.

"But it is more than that." He enveloped her in his embrace, misting her forehead, her eyelids, her cheeks with gentle kisses. "You are very smart and very strong. I want you to bear my children."

She looked shocked.

He continued, "I want to care for you all the days of my life."

Cami's lovely eyes shone with tears. Sniffling, she bent her forehead so she leaned against his shoulder.

He couldn't help his urgency. He had to know. "So you'll say yes?"

Drawing back, Cami pressed trembling hands to her cheeks. Though she'd dreamed of this moment, the reality was so scary that she couldn't say yes.

But could she possibly say no? Ray made her feel things she'd never felt—wonderful, magical sensations she didn't want to do without. She'd grown to crave that marvelous tingle that ran up and down her back when she saw him. Heck, she sizzled just when she thought about him. And when they were together, the yearning ache multiplied exponentially. She hungered for it, and him, like an addict longs for his next fix.

And she wanted more.

She knew there was more. She was inexperienced, not ignorant. She'd read *Playgirl* and *Cosmo,* listened to the gossip of other women and taken sex education in school. She knew what men and women did together, and she wanted to do it, too.

Now she'd met someone she desired, respected, trusted and loved. Someone who offered her the commitment she demanded as the price for her innocence.

She inhaled a deep breath and let it out slowly while contemplating Ray.

His gaze drank her in as though she were very hot, strong coffee and he really needed his morning caffeine.

He seemed sincere. *I want to care for you all the days of my life.*

She couldn't ask for a sweeter proposal.

"Yes," she whispered.

"What?"

"Yes! Yes! Yes! Yes!" She grabbed his robe and, heedless of the diamond ring he clutched in one hand, began to twirl him around the room, laughing.

Dancing with her, he somehow managed to pull the ring from the box and jam it on her finger. "A perfect fit," he gloated.

"But of course." She imitated his accent, waving her hand in the air. The diamond caught the faint starlight, winking and glittering. "It would not dare to defy a prince of Adnan!"

He grabbed her hand and pulled her against him. His chest felt marvelously hard and solid against her breasts. He kissed her, first nibbling tenderly at her lips. After she opened to him, he made love to her mouth until he'd stolen every wisp of oxygen from her body, leaving her breathless and panting for him.

He smiled at her. "Well, then. We must get ready to go."

"Go? Go where?"

"To get married."

"Now?" She tipped her head to one side.

He stroked her cheekbone with a gentle fingertip. "Now."

"Tonight?"

"Yes, tonight."

"Why so soon?"

"I do not want you to get away or change your mind."

"Hey, I love you. I won't change." Hurt, Cami wondered how Ray could think she wouldn't be true. She'd do anything to soothe his fears, including elope. Why not? She was sure of her love.

"All right. I admit it. I wish to get lucky very soon." He gave her his rogue's grin.

Tiny shivers zipped up and down her spine. "But what should I tell my father? He hasn't been well."

"What is the problem?"

"His asthma."

Ray released her. "I know he is very important to you. What did you tell him about tonight?"

"I told him I'm having dinner out with the man I'm dating."

"Oh? And what have you told him about me?" Ray regarded her with curious eyes.

Did she detect a little nervousness? Well, that was

natural. "Not much, just that you're older and wanted an exclusive relationship. He thought that was okay, but he didn't want details about, um, us."

He scratched his ear, looking thoughtful. "If he does not want details, then we need not provide them, especially if he has been unwell."

Cami pursed her lips. "I bet Dad wants a big church wedding."

"That will take a long time to arrange, will it not?" Ray frowned.

"Yes." She fiddled with her braid.

"Cami, since we are sure, let's just do it. We can have the big ceremony when your father is again healthy. We can, what is it called, renew our vows later, can we not?"

Chapter Seven

After Ray changed into jeans and Cami packed her still-damp lingerie into her handbag, he bundled her into the truck.

"How on earth are you going to arrange a wedding at such short notice?" Cami asked. "And where are we going?"

"Do not worry," he said, smiling. "Do not worry about anything."

They drove all night, with Cami falling asleep along the way. Arriving at the port of Galveston at dawn, she rubbed her eyes, then stared at the white metal wall of the ship looming above.

Then she understood. "We're going on a cruise, and the captain's gonna marry us! Oh, Ray, you're a genius!" She flung her arms around Ray's neck and pressed a big, smacking kiss on his mouth.

He grinned. "I'd already booked the cruise and made the arrangements, hoping you'd say yes. We will be able to marry when the ship sails into international waters.''

"Where are we going?''

"It is only a short cruise, since you do not have your passport. We go to New Orleans, and visit beaches along the way to and fro.''

"How long will we be gone?''

"Three days.''

Cami bit her lip, worrying about the consequences of her misadventure. "I really oughtta call Dad.''

"Cami, it is dawn. You cannot call your father now. He will be asleep.'' Ray gestured. "Let us go aboard the ship. It is early, but I will talk with the purser and see if our suite is ready. You can call home at a more civilized hour.''

"Suite?''

"Why, yes. I booked the honeymoon suite, of course.'' He winked at her.

"Oh, my God!'' Cami clapped an excited hand to her mouth.

Taking her arm, Rayhan guided Cami up the gangplank, praying she wouldn't get to a phone until after they'd left port. If she did, he bet Old Man Ellison would talk her out of the elopement. And if Ellison learned the identity of Cami's suitor before they were wed and their marriage consummated, Rayhan would wager his fastest Arabian that the union would be annulled before sundown.

No, he had to keep Cami away from a telephone until she was wedded, thoroughly bedded and, hopefully, pregnant. At the same time, he couldn't appear to obstruct her.

After talking with the two sailors at the top of the gangplank, and slipping each a fifty, Rayhan led Cami into the ship's salon, which resembled a hotel lobby. "See, Cami. If our room isn't ready, we can have breakfast. Then it should be time to call home." He pointed at a bank of phones near a rest room.

She looked relieved.

"Do not worry." Rayhan injected a good dose of reassurance into his voice. "All will be well. Your father may be surprised when he hears the news, but not displeased, I hope?"

She turned to him. "That's what I'm afraid of. I've never done much of anything without talking it over with Dad."

Fear ripped through him, the stress wrenching his gut into knots. Tugging her arm, he went to a sofa and sat with her. "Cami, if you are not sure, we shouldn't—"

"Oh, I'm sure! I just feel that I should tell him."

"Of course you should." Rayhan made a mental note to call his ranch first and arrange something—anything—to get Charles Ellison away from the phone when his daughter called, or perhaps to keep the line engaged until they'd married.

Cami looked at her watch. "It's six o'clock. Even if Dad isn't awake, Robbie will be. She's our housekeeper. She gets up early to cook for the hands." She pulled a cellular phone from her handbag and began to poke buttons.

Rayhan relaxed. He'd met Roberta Morris several times in McMahon, occasionally exchanging a few words with her. He knew she'd been hired by Charles

Ellison a couple of years after Rayhan purchased his ranch. Robbie had never shown, by word or deed, she was aware of any strain between the denizens of the Double Eagle and the C-Bar-C.

"Hi, Robbie, it's Cami."

"Cami! Where are you?" The connection wasn't great, but Cami could hear Robbie over the static.

"I'm out with a friend. Is Dad up yet?" Cami smiled at Ray, who watched her. One of his eyelids twitched.

Robbie said, "No, he had a bad night. He won't be up for an hour or so. Out with a friend? Where?"

Cami hesitated. "Hold on, okay?" She covered the receiver and said to Ray, "I don't want Dad to hear from Robbie that I'm getting married. We should tell him. So what should I say?"

"Tell her everything is all right. You had an unexpected opportunity to travel to New Orleans with a friend, and decided to go. You'll be back Thursday."

"Okay." Cami, relieved, realized that everything should be fine. She was an adult, wasn't she? Her father had raised her to make decisions for herself. Besides, he'd never gotten really mad at her for anything she'd done, not even when, at age eleven, she'd gone joyriding in one of the ranch's trucks and crashed it into a tree.

So she relayed the message to Robbie. The housekeeper said, "I'll tell your father. Thanks for calling in, Cami. Otherwise we'd worry."

After ending the conversation, Cami clicked off her phone and smiled at Ray. "Glad I got that done. Now let's go eat."

Ray had arranged a relaxing day for Cami, so after breakfast he dropped her off at the ship's spa. Following a two-hour massage and a light lunch, Cami, feeling delightfully pampered, had her face made up, her fingernails painted and her feet pedicured. Then the salon stylist washed and braided her blond hair into a coronet, the coiffure Cami wanted for the wedding ceremony.

The ceremony. Cami's heart did backflips when she contemplated what would happen at six o'clock that night. Squelching her nerves, she visited the row of shops on the ship's main deck. "Buy whatever you need," Ray had said. "Including a dress for tonight. Charge it to the room."

The *Corsair,* a fully outfitted luxury liner of the Caravel Cruise Line, boasted everything, including a bridal boutique. In a reasonably short time, Cami bought a dress, heels and a veil.

Her wedding dress. She picked a white silk sheath with a beaded, wrapped bodice. It fell straight to her ankles from the empire waist, with its long skirt skimming her hips.

Though the dress left her arms bare and plunged below her collarbones to a vee, it outlined rather than exposed her body. She hoped Ray, who she knew had a prudish streak, would like it.

A cabin attendant showed Cami, clutching several shopping bags, to the honeymoon suite. When she saw the room, her muscles slackened, allowing her parcels to fall to the carpeted floor.

A big, round bed on a dais dominated the suite. Her mouth went dry and her flesh shivered at the sight. She imagined herself and Ray, naked and en-twined, on its flaming-red satin comforter.

She took a deep breath, steadying herself, then looked around the room.

Ray had apparently come and gone, leaving her a lavish bouquet of two dozen yellow roses, a gift-wrapped box and a note.

> My dearest Cami,
> I hope you enjoyed your day. I am told that Americans believe it is bad fortune for the bride and groom to meet before the ceremony. So we will see each other again in the ship's chapel at six.
>
> In the meantime, please accept my wedding gift.
>
> Missing you every moment,
R.

Cami examined the note for a long time, realizing this was the first time she'd seen Ray's handwriting. It held none of the hesitancy she supposed a for-eigner's penmanship might; rather the confident strokes reflected Ray's bold personality.

Then she turned her attention to her present. She tore the silver wrapping paper from the package and discovered diamond stud earrings and a necklace that matched her engagement ring. The gifts were opulent, yet simple and modest. How like Ray, Cami thought. Better, they'd look wonderful with her dress.

Smiling, Cami fingered the platinum chain from which a heart-shaped diamond hung, glad she'd also purchased Ray a keepsake. She'd bought a chunky, masculine bracelet in gold, and had asked the jeweler to engrave the flat, square clasp.

She tried again to phone her father to share her joy, but the C-Bar-C's line was busy. Darn.

Six o'clock came. Cami, quivering with excitement, slipped her feet into her new white satin pumps and walked to the chapel. Calm but expectant, she wondered if anyone she passed in the corridors could see her pounding pulse, hear the eager beat of her heart, divine the inner joy that infused every cell of her body.

She approached the chapel's wooden double doors. A smiling woman introduced herself as the ship's activities director, then gave Cami a bouquet of yellow roses. Cami buried her face in the fragrant blooms to inhale deeply. Ray was so-o-o-o romantic.

Her resolve to wed this unique, special man, already firm, hardened into granite. Though he'd never told her he loved her, everything he did reflected his sincerity and devotion. Men didn't expose their romantic souls unless they were sure. Cami was certain she'd found the steadfast, true love she craved, now and for the rest of her life.

After helping Cami with her veil, the activities director opened the double doors. Cami blinked, dazzled by the glittering lights. She heard the trill of a sweet violin playing.

Cami's gaze traveled the length of the central aisle toward Ray, standing straight and proud against a backdrop of yellow roses, red gladiolus and white mums. He also wore white, his tux setting off his exotic, dark good looks. Her mind spun. After a few seconds she reminded herself to breathe, but it was tough. Her man was a hottie, and just looking at him sucked the wind right out of her lungs.

She practically sprinted down the aisle to stand by his side.

Chapter Eight

Champagne corks and flashbulbs popped, startling Cami, already dizzied by the brief yet solemn ceremony.

She'd joined her life to Ray's. She was married.

Playing with the stem of her champagne flute, she watched him covertly as he finished taking care of the arrangements with the captain and the photographer. Ray's broad shoulders, handsomely filling out the tux; his long, graceful hands, hands that could take her to heaven and back; his muscular, well-proportioned body, which would soon make her a woman...his wife.

When he returned to her side, her gaze traveled to his face. Though often dark and guarded, at this moment his open smile and relaxed eyes concealed nothing. Certain she'd done the right thing, Cami placed her hand in her husband's for the walk back to their suite.

At the door, Ray hefted her in his arms.

"Oh, come on," Cami said. "That's so-o-o-o corny."

"I am told it is good luck. Do you not want the best fortune can offer? Come." Ray tucked her against him with a secure grip. "Oh, Cami. I forgot. The card key to this room is in my jacket pocket."

"The side pocket?"

"No, the inner one. Get it for me, will you?"

Instead of reaching into the inner pocket, Cami shoved her hand between two of the studs of his shirt and ran her fingernails across his chest. She found his nipple and rimmed it, scratching gently.

Staggering, Ray ground out something guttural in Arabic she didn't understand.

"What did you just say?"

"Never mind. Where did you learn to do that?"

She gave him her sauciest grin and wiggled her bottom against him. Ray's grip slackened; he nearly dropped her.

Cami giggled. "In a women's magazine."

"Please get the key, Cami. Now."

She opened the door and he managed to jockey her through it without hitting her head or her heels against either jamb. "You did that very well," she said.

"I have never before done such a foolish thing. Are there many other arcane American customs which we must perform before we may get lucky?"

She shook her head. "Nope, we've done them all."

"Yes, we have, haven't we?" He swung her around. "We did it, Cami, we really did it!"

Exultant laughter burst from her chest and bubbled

through her throat, filling her with happiness. "Yeah, we sure did! We got married!"

Ray peppered her forehead, eyelids, nose and cheeks with light little kisses before carefully setting her on her feet. She kissed back, trying to take him deeper into the seduction she anticipated and welcomed.

But Ray evidently had other ideas. After slipping off his jacket, he crossed the room to tinker with the suite's music system. Soon a jazz singer crooned a sultry ballad. Ray again opened his arms to her, and she slid within his embrace, fitting there as though they'd been designed for each other.

While they danced, she feathered her lips over his, teasing and tempting, eager to truly become his. Their kisses grew deeper and more searching. Cami let her hands roam over Ray's chest, loosening his tie, plucking at the studs holding his shirt together, uncinching his cummerbund. She let it drop to the floor.

She didn't know what had gotten into her. Some wanton, sex-crazed devil-wench had taken over her body, filling it with an uncontrollable heat and need. She couldn't keep her hands off Ray.

And he sure wasn't resisting her. Instead he pressed her head closer to him when she bent to rub her face in his rough, masculine mat of chest hair. She circled one of his dark nipples with her tongue, then scraped it with her teeth into an aroused point. He moaned and murmured something in Arabic, his hand tightening on her nape.

Cami discovered she liked to turn on her husband, but she was selfish enough to want this consummation for herself. She wanted to see everything, feel everything, do everything—

A knock at the door interrupted her, startling her away from her frantic exploration of Ray's torso.

He smiled at her as he answered the door, swinging it wide. "Dinner has arrived."

Dinner! Cami didn't want dinner. She wanted Ray. She tapped her toe on the carpet as the servers unloaded the feast onto a nearby table: caviar on toast points, lobster bisque, grilled baby prawns with baby new potatoes, and a salad of fresh baby greens.

"Hmmm," she said as the servers left. "Is there a message in this supper?"

"I beg your pardon?" Ray poured two glasses of water and set them beside their plates.

"Eggs." She pointed at the caviar. "Baby prawns. Baby potatoes. Baby greens. Eggs and babies. You got an agenda here, honey?"

He grinned and dipped his head. A lock of dark hair fell appealingly across his forehead. "I am not becoming any younger, Cami. I realize in this country that women have a choice, and I believe that is right. But I hope you choose to bear children for us, to complete our lives."

She breathed in deeply, then exhaled, trying to find her center. "I don't know, Ray—"

"If you are not sure about things, then you shouldn't."

"Oh, I'm sure about us. I love you. Why do you doubt that?" Crossing the room to him, she laid her head on his chest. His beautiful, naked chest.

"I know everything has happened so fast. If you have doubts, I cannot blame you, my wife."

"My wife." She sighed. "Those have got to be the two most beautiful words in the English language, except for maybe my husband." She looked up into his face, reading anxiety in his dark eyes.

Cami couldn't bear for him to suffer a moment's worry. "I have no doubts. Let's make a baby."

Taking his hand, she led him to their bed.

Wakeful even at 2:00 a.m., Rayhan sat up in bed and glanced at his sleeping wife. Even in her rest, a smile curved Cami's lips.

He didn't want his restlessness to disturb her, so he carefully slid from between the rumpled sheets, then tugged on his jeans. He placed a single yellow rose in the dent his head had left in the pillow beside her before taking the room key and leaving the suite.

After cadging a cigarette from a sailor, Rayhan wandered over to a dark corner of the deck. Relaxing into a lounge chair, he tilted his head back to marvel at the absolute blackness of the night sky at sea, lit only by faraway pinpoints of infinite stars. Their abundant, shimmering glitter, a lavish diamond necklace on the bosom of the queen of heaven, reminded him of lovemaking with his wife.

His wife.

Everything about her shocked him, staggered him, drew him deeper into the web she'd woven with her innocent body and wise smiles, her ardent eyes and curious hands.

She'd been all maidenly modesty during their wed-

ding ceremony. Robed in white like a virginal priest-
ess, she'd spoken the words of the ancient ritual with
solemnity, inspiring from him the same reverence.

Rayhan had meant every word of his vows.

Then later he'd carried her across the threshold of
the honeymoon suite. Neither managed to eat much
of the dinner he'd ordered. The champagne had gone
flat, and the caviar remained uneaten.

They'd preferred to devour each other.

Intensely aware of the importance of Cami's first
time, he'd tried to ease into sex gradually. This night
would set the pattern for their lovemaking for years
to come. He'd guided his wife to the peak of passion
before allowing himself release into pleasure, knowing that a bad experience for Cami would be a disaster.

He needn't have worried. *Lovemaking* was a mild
word for what happened between them. Rayhan
closed his eyes, remembering the words of the traditional wedding ceremony. *With my body, I thee wor-
ship.*

They'd worshipped each other the way pagans wor-
ship a wild fertility goddess.

Rayhan drew deeply on the cigarette, dragging its
smoke into his mouth. He touched the ring he wore
on his left hand, then fondled the bracelet she'd given
him. Running his finger over the engraved clasp, he
caressed the incised letters: C+R. Cami and Rayhan.
His heart swelled into his throat.

He looked up into the heavens, thanking Whoever
dwelt there for his good fortune, for he was surely
the luckiest husband in the world.

* * *

The door closed with a click, followed by the rustle of movement, alerting Cami to Ray's return. Then she felt him slip into bed, his long, cool body flowing like water next to hers.

"Where did you go on our honeymoon night?" she asked sleepily. "Bad hubby!" She smacked him lightly on one hip.

His deep chuckle rolled over her in the darkness before he grabbed her wrists and trapped them above her head. With a gasp, Cami involuntarily arched her back. She tried to pull away from his grip.

He didn't let go, but chuckled again. "Relax, my darling. Let me compensate you for my offense." He rolled, his weight pinning her hips onto the mattress.

Lips stroked her face, her neck…lower. Much lower.

Her body started to quiver with delighted anticipation. In perfect trust, Cami gave herself to her husband and his love.

They skipped the excursion to one of the beaches lining the Gulf Coast, preferring to spend the day in bed. The next morning the ship docked at New Orleans. They played tourist, first exploring a haunted mansion in the Garden District, then visiting the zoo and the aquarium. They attended an "authentic voodoo ritual" that made Cami giggle, embarrassing them so much they had to leave.

Still chuckling over the spectacle his wife had made, Rayhan treated Cami to a delicious Creole dinner. They ate crawfish étouffée and drank the wonderful New Orleans chicory-laced coffee.

After the ship left New Orleans that night, the captain announced that due to a spot of rough weather, the *Corsair* had to change course and head farther out to sea.

Cami wasn't much of a sailor, and Rayhan eyed her with worry as she collapsed onto their bed. "As you Americans might say, you look a tad green about the gills."

Abruptly, she stood, shoved past him and dashed into the bathroom. Following, Rayhan found her bent over the sink, groaning as the remains of crawfish étouffée went down the drain.

"Oh, darling." He ran the cold water tap. "Here, rinse your mouth."

Cami complied, moaning weakly. He grabbed a clean washcloth and drenched it with water. After wringing it out, he pressed it to her forehead.

It occurred to him that he'd never gone to so much trouble over another person. For his horses, yes, he sacrificed, staying up nights to watch a sick colt or a pregnant mare. But another human being? A woman?

Rayhan frowned as he led his wife back to bed. After urging her to lie down, he placed the cold compress onto her brow and hunted for a basin in case she again became ill.

He'd never troubled himself over bedmates. As a prince of Adnan, they were ever present in his youth. In Paris, where he'd attended school, the Frenchwomen kept him amused but not distracted from his studies. Later he'd enjoyed his share of American girls.

But he'd married only one woman.

Marriage has little to do with emotion, he reminded himself. Royals selected their mates for tangible qualities, not for love. He'd picked Cami because she was wealthy, intelligent and beautiful, an unsullied vessel for his seed and a worthy mother for his children.

That she was lovable hadn't entered into his decision making, and didn't have to now, or ever. That he loved her was impossible. Ridiculous. Love was a fantasy told to timorous virgins to lure them into bed or marriage. Love was a fool's dream.

He hadn't fallen in love with his wife. He'd married her to restore honor and complete his revenge upon her swindling father.

Jolted, Rayhan realized he hadn't thought about Charles Ellison, honor, or revenge for a long time.

But that didn't mean he'd fallen in love with his wife, though he quite liked his beautiful Texan princess. He'd keep and enjoy her for as long as possible.

He avoided thinking deeply about the twist their marriage would surely take upon their return to Mc-Mahon. As his wife, Cami would live at the Double Eagle. Rayhan decided she'd simply have to adjust to a more distant relationship with her father.

"What is this?" Standing at the purser's desk, Ray, brow creased, scrutinized the bill for their cruise. Cami slipped an arm around his waist and peeked over his shoulder at the paper, wondering what had annoyed her usually unflappable husband.

"I'm sure it's correct, sir." The young man behind the desk anxiously shoved back a forelock of sandy hair.

Ray turned to her. "Camille. I do not see the charges for your clothes. How is that possible?"

Cami grinned at him. Now that the storm had passed and the ship had docked, she was back to her accustomed cheerful spirits. "I put everything on my credit cards."

"You are my wife. You do not need to spend your funds."

She put her lips near his ear. "I didn't want you to think I married you for your money, honey. I'm a wealthy woman, you know." She nibbled on his lobe.

Passing a hand around her waist, he eased Cami closer. "That may be, but I am capable of clothing my wife." His fingertips drew a line up her back to her nape, then made little circles there. She shivered with renewed desire.

Glad he didn't seem to care about her net worth, she said, "Ray, I wasn't going to let you buy your own wedding present." She fingered the heavy gold bracelet circling his wrist.

He caught her hand and kissed it. "Very well, my darling. We will not argue about these trifles. But in the future, shall we not discuss these matters before-hand?"

"But of course, prince. I would not dream of dis-obeying a sheikh of Adnan." She delighted in imi-tating his accent.

He frowned and wrinkled his nose.

Cami giggled.

The ship had docked at dawn. Despite the early hour, Cami wanted to rush home to share her happiness with her father. She hurried Ray into his truck and didn't want to stop along the way. However, she couldn't help noticing that the closer they drove to McMahon, the quieter Ray became.

As he turned off the main road and headed toward their ranches, his hands held the steering wheel in a death grip, knuckles white.

"What's wrong?" She placed a hand over his tight fingers.

Ray sighed. "I am afraid your father will not approve of what we have done."

Her heart thudded dully. "So am I. We were pretty impulsive. But I'm sure about us. Aren't you?"

"Absolutely," he said at once. "Cami, whatever may happen, let us remember that we are sure. No regrets, all right?"

"No regrets."

Guessing her father would be at work, Cami took Ray's hand and led him through her home to the study. Sure enough, Charles sat behind his desk, talking on the telephone. When Cami entered, Ray in tow, her dad's eyes became hooded and murky. He said into the handset, "Hey, Larry. Something's come up. Talk to ya later."

Cami's father clicked off the phone and set it on the desk. An indefinable expression entered his watery blue eyes. His gaze shifted from Cami to Ray.

Cami stared. For the first time in her life, her father showed fear, and…guilt? What was going on?

Ray cleared his throat. "Hello, old friend." Acid edged his tone.

Old friend? What did Ray mean? Did her father and her husband have a connection they'd never mentioned to her? "You two know each other?" she asked.

"Not at all." Ray's voice sounded cool, even distant.

Weirder and weirder.

"We've had some dealings in the past." Charles's glance cut to her left hand, placed on Ray's arm. "Cami, what is that?"

Cami proudly displayed her new rings. Though she adored the heart-shaped diamond, she loved their wedding set more. Of gold and platinum filigree, the flowing Arabic characters on each ring spelled out a vow of faithfulness. Or so Ray had said. "These are my engagement and wedding rings. We're married. We got married three days ago on a cruise to New Orleans."

Grabbing a cane set close to the desk, Charles stood. "Cami, why didn't you talk to me?" he croaked.

Cami could hear his tight, short, angry breaths. "I, uh, I..." She cast a desperate glance at Ray. Her father's reaction overshadowed her worst expectations. He appeared on the verge of shock, not joy.

Ray's face and eyes now looked as though they'd been carved out of obsidian. Cami had expected her suave husband to smile, shake her father's hand, maybe even ask for his blessing. Instead Ray did nothing, while Cami's tongue stuck to the roof of her dry mouth, her voice trapped by a dawning sense of horror.

"So you did it." Charles wheezed, his gaze pinned on Ray. "You couldn't get your greedy hands on the oil ten years ago. So you stole my little girl and married her money." Limping with the cane in hand, he drew closer. "You lousy, gold-digging skunk."

Ray emitted a short, contemptuous laugh. "Gold-digging. Ha. I do not wish to boast, but I could buy and sell this town, and both of you, several times over."

"So what was the point?" Charles had hobbled to within a yard of Cami, who still clutched her husband's arm. Her father's lips had turned pale, even bluish.

Ray shrugged. "Honor. Vengeance." He fixed Cami with an enigmatic gaze. "Desire. I have need of a wife. She is most precious to you, is she not? And now she is mine."

Cami's heart forgot how to beat. *I have need of a wife.* That was cold, ice-cold. Ray had never said he loved her, and she'd let that omission slide. She'd told herself that he showed her his love by his acts, rather than by expressing it verbally.

Had she hidden the truth from herself? "What is this all about?" she managed to whisper through her taut, tense throat.

Charles raised his cane and swung it at Ray's head. He took the glancing blow on an upraised arm, then yanked the weapon from Charles's grasp, flinging it aside.

Cami's father fell against her, then toppled to the

floor, limbs convulsing. He jerked a twitching hand in the direction of his desk, choking out, "My medicine!"

"Oh, my God!" Cami screamed. "He's having an asthma attack!" She raced to his desk drawer and wrenched it open, scrabbling for her father's inhaler.

Grabbing the phone, Ray punched three buttons before beginning to talk in a tight, terse voice.

Sirens screaming, an ambulance with paramedics showed up, just a few minutes after Ray called 911. They stabilized Charles, then took him to the hospital. Because she knew everyone in McMahon, including the paramedics, Cami rode along with her father. The oxygen mask over his face didn't allow conversation, so Cami's mind remained a whirlpool of questions, and her heart a maelstrom of conflicting emotions.

When Charles was placed in a cubicle, Cami lingered by his side until he could speak. Ray had stayed in the waiting room, because only one visitor at a time was allowed in the E.R.

"Dad, can you talk to me? Can you tell me what's going on with you and Ray?"

Charles sighed. "Oh, Cami. This mess is all my fault. Can you forgive me?"

"I don't know that there's anything to forgive. What happened?"

Rayhan leaned against a doorpost, occasionally sipping from a cup of the awful vending-machine coffee. He watched Cami enter the waiting room from the E.R. and approach.

For a moment he felt like a puppet on a stage, strings tugged by an invisible master. Then he reminded himself that he'd created the situation and had to live with it.

His wife had aged in the past few hours, transforming from a carefree girl to a saddened woman. Her shoulders drooped. Her feet dragged. Her teary eyes appeared red and ravaged.

He briefly closed his eyes. He'd never thought about how his actions would affect the woman to whom he'd committed his life.

He was a fool.

Finally she stood before him. He offered her the coffee.

Cami passed her nose over the rim of the cup, sniffing. She winced, then blew on the surface of the steamy beverage. "Ray, is it true?"

"What?"

"My father swindled you out of a fortune ten years ago." Her blue eyes steadily regarded him over the rim of the cup. "*My* fortune."

Rayhan breathed in and out, aware of his sighing inhalations; her eyelashes, spiky with her salt tears; the importance of the moment.

His revenge did not taste sweet but was flavored by a most bitter brew: guilt. He'd hurt her. Though that had been necessary, he wanted her to understand.

He said, "That is my opinion, yes. I was very young—about your age—and my English was not good." He gestured. "As you know, it still is not perfect. The king, my father, assigned to me the royal Adnani attorney, who did not understand the situation, either. Your father said things about the deed that turned out to be false. I could not drill for oil on my land. I still cannot.''

''And you've plotted revenge ever since.'' Her voice dropped to a whisper. ''That's sick.''

How could she think such a terrible thing? She was his wife! ''We said no regrets. Did we not?'' He reached out to touch her shoulder.

Cami jerked away. ''That was before I learned how twisted you are.'' She turned and walked out of the hospital without a single look back at him.

He wanted to run after her, explain everything, but what was there to explain?

Indecisive, Rayhan shifted, back and forth, left boot to right and back again. Cami was very angry and distressed over the situation. Yes, that was it. Perhaps he would be wiser to wait. She would come back to him of her own accord, once she had calmed down and thought matters through. If she did not—Rayhan's heart froze in his chest.

Then, taking deep, even breaths, he firmed his resolve. If she did not return to him, she did not believe in their wedding vows. If so, he would not beg her. If she did not believe in their marriage, they had nothing.

Chapter Nine

Dear Dad:
I've rented an apartment in San Antonio and will start school again in September. I know I left the ranch really quickly after you got out of the hospital, and I'm sorry. But please understand why I can't stay with you anymore. I just need some time to myself to sort things out.

Cami

Syed, capital city of Adnan
Three weeks later

Rayhan's eldest brother, the king, paced up and down the tiled colonnade with jerky strides, his robes swinging. "This is a disaster!" He waved the sheaf of faxes he held. "Your wife has filed for divorce! She refuses the summons of a prince of Adnan!"

Rayhan grimaced. To Kadar, everything was a disaster. He had always been so. Cami would have labelled his brother a "drama mama," in her charming slang. "She is an American," Rayhan said prosaically. "She does not have to obey my command."

"She must." The king resumed his pacing. "The situation is very unsettled. The anti-American sentiment in the desert tribes will be inflamed by her insolence. They will seek to push us closer to the foreign extremists and their insanities."

Rayhan shuddered. No Adnani—except for the ever-fractious desert tribes—wanted their peaceful country to go the violent way of the extremists in neighboring countries. "What can be done?"

"You will not consider marrying Matana al-Qamra? Her family will be gravely insulted if you back out of the wedding. They are rumored to desire an alliance with the desert tribes to incite revolution."

"Absolutely not." Rayhan crossed his arms over his chest. "I am already married."

"Adnani law permits royal princes to take multiple wives."

"The engagement was negotiated without my agreement," Rayhan snapped. "I will not be a political pawn." He knew if he bent on this matter, his life would never be his own. Besides, he didn't want another bad marriage.

"All of us are political pawns!"

"You married for love." Rayhan nodded toward

his pregnant sister-in-law, the queen, who reclined upon a chaise at the far end of the courtyard.

The king's stern face softened as he gazed at his wife. "That is true, but Habiba and I were affianced when we were children. We grew to love each other over the years. Even if it had not been so, we would have married for the stability of the country. And that is what you must do!"

"No."

"You are refusing a direct command?"

Rayhan glared at his brother, knowing the king could have him beheaded in the central square of Syed if the monarch so chose. "*You* marry her if it is so important."

"I cannot. Habiba is in a very delicate condition. You are minister without portfolio, and already engaged to Matana. Do something!"

In the past month Rayhan had learned that his job as minister without portfolio meant that he was responsible for everything, yet had power over nothing.

"I can travel to Texas and ask my wife to visit. If she is cooperative, her presence may stabilize the situation." That would accomplish much. He missed Texas, his horses and his land. He hated the idea of begging Cami for anything, but he had to admit that he yearned for her.

Nothing had gone right for Rayhan since they'd stepped off the cruise boat. Now he wished they'd stayed on the ship and sailed away to forever.

When Cami had been near, his heart had brimmed with happiness. Without her, even the bright Adnani sunshine seemed tarnished and dark around the edges. He'd returned to his homeland to make a fresh start, but nothing worked, nothing was right.

"No, no," said the king. "You cannot demean yourself or our family. That will damage our position with the people. I will send someone to bring her here."

Rayhan stirred. "She must remain unharmed."

"But of course. She is your wife, the consort of a prince of Adnan. But she must come."

Tucking the morning paper under her arm, Cami walked with leaden feet out of her apartment. After locking the door, she slowly made her way down the stairs and into the street. Despite her light summer dress, the August heat punched her like a fist.

As time had dragged on, she'd felt worse and worse. She prayed she wasn't pregnant, but she had the symptoms: sick a lot, couldn't keep anything down, wanted to stay in bed all day long.

A pregnancy would be catastrophic. She remembered her friend Jenelle's misery: nineteen, pregnant and stuck in a bad marriage. Tightening her mouth, Cami squared her shoulders and marched down the sidewalk. That wouldn't happen to her. She'd already filed for divorce, and if the store-bought pregnancy test revealed she was expecting, she'd deal with it.

If and when she gathered the courage to use the test.

She entered the Java Joint on the corner. She liked to drink an iced white chocolate mocha there every morning while reading the paper. Today she noticed a new employee mixing up the coffee drinks, an older fellow whose dark good looks reminded her of Ray.

She turned her head, hating anything that resembled her low-down, two-faced rat of a husband. She paid for her drink, then took it and her paper to a table near the window.

Sipping, she tried to read the paper, but her scrambled brain couldn't focus. She rubbed her temple. Her runaway train of thought would get her nowhere. She'd traveled on the same mental track over and over in the past weeks. Nothing seemed to erase the chaos running riot in her mind and heart.

Her guilt over hurting her father. Her fury toward both Charles and Ray. Her father should have told her everything years before, she reminded herself. Instead, he'd kept information germane to the sale of the Double Eagle from her.

After leaving the hospital, Cami had returned to her ranch to check the deed. A clause labeled "Grant of Mineral Rights," written in confusing language with tiny type, excluded the oil lying under both the C-Bar-C and the Double Eagle. A careless reader—or a young man with poor English—would have been misled, if not tricked.

She couldn't wrap her mind around the word *swindle* in connection with her father, who'd always cared for her so tenderly. But did Dad's acts justify what Ray had done?

Cami winced. Ray had deceived her, married her for revenge and taken her innocence for the lowest of motives. *She is most precious to you, is she not? And now she is mine.* The snake had married her only to hurt her father, as though she were nothing but a pawn for his sick games. Now he had the gall to summon her to Adnan, for some kind of royal whoop-te-do. Yeah, right.

He'd made a complete dupe of her. Every conclusion she'd reached about him—that he was honest, cared about her and not her fortune—had been dead wrong. Not only was she angry at Ray, but she was furious at herself. How could she have been such a fool?

She sucked iced coffee through the straw, hoping to cool her useless rage, then flipped through the paper to the entertainment section. She needed a diversion. A movie would do the trick.

The movie listings were printed in the tiniest of fonts. Squinting, Cami dropped her head until her nose was touching the paper, but still the words seemed to wobble and drift across her field of vision, finally growing completely dark.

Cramped and stiff, with a queasy headache reminiscent of her seasickness, Cami awakened in what appeared to be a very peculiar bedroom. Trying to ignore her nausea, she rubbed sleep out of her gummy eyes while deciphering her surroundings.

Everything seemed to have been designed for dwarves. Her long body, still clothed in her now-crumpled pink dress, had been crammed into a narrow bunk. Only a flattened foam pillow cradled her head.

The odd, trapezoidal room had rounded windows sized for fairies or elves.

Cami tore off the confining sheet and thin blanket, then gasped at the slap of cool air. She became aware of a subliminal hum buzzing at the outer edges of her consciousness.

She stood. The room tipped and twirled. Stumbling to one of the elfin windows, she saw blue sky and puffy clouds, with a sparkling ocean glittering far, far below.

"That skunk!" She never wanted to see Ray again, but if she did, she'd skin him alive and then stomp on him with her cowboy boots. She'd ignored his imperious summons, so he'd had her kidnapped!

The timbre of the engines changed. The plane swayed, tilted, then stabilized. Cami dashed for one of the doors, praying she'd picked the lavatory.

Rayhan watched Cami shake her arm free of one of her guards. She stumbled down the ramp out of the king's private jet.

His wife looked like a ragamuffin. Her hair had escaped sloppy plaits. Though a modest calf length, her loose pink dress showed wrinkle upon wrinkle, as if she'd slept in it. It hung on her slender, wraith-like frame. Had she lost weight?

She came closer. He could see purplish crescents staining the thin skin beneath her eyes, which themselves seemed droopy and dulled.

The king's agents who'd accompanied her didn't look much better. One sported a black eye. The *thobe* of another was stained brown. As the group drew near, Rayhan deduced from the smell that the agent had been the target of his wife's morning coffee, hurled by her enraged hand.

One of the guards took her arm to help her down the ramp. Flinging his hand away, she elbowed him in the side, snarling, "Don't touch me!"

The king's agents couldn't match her long, jerky strides. She marched toward Rayhan, showing not a trace of the fear a lesser woman would exhibit in the same situation, finding herself abducted to a strange land. Rayhan felt his chest puff with pride. His wife had the heart of a lioness.

Now only a foot away, she reached for the front of his *thobe*. Tugging on his clothing, she drew him near, as if to embrace him. Rayhan's heart leaped. Perhaps all was well.

As he prepared to greet his wife with his heartiest kiss, she used one finger to turn his head.

He felt her lips approach his ear. His skin tingled at the puff of her breath.

"You lowdown, scheming skunk!" she screamed directly into his ear.

Yanking away, Rayhan winced. He guessed he deserved whatever punishment she meted, but at the same time, she had to understand her position in their society. Removing her hands from his *thobe,* he said calmly, "The penalty for assaulting a member of the Adnani royal family is death by beheading."

*   *   *

The first thing Cami noticed were the colors of Adnan. Undimmed by even a hint of humidity, utterly clear and dustless, the air shimmered with a brilliant white sun that lit everything with unnatural vividness. The sky wasn't merely blue or even cerulean, but a bright hard cobalt that hammered at her, so vibrant it hurt.

Flags were everywhere, and the national colors reflected the intense light. A field of yellow, piercing as hot curry, lay beneath a horizontal center stripe of emerald. The dazzling blue of the Adnani sky topped the yellow and green. The colors tore at her eyes, accentuating her nausea and dizziness.

The heat didn't help, either, and when Ray took her arm to lead her into an air-conditioned limousine, Cami didn't resist. Instead she breathed a gusty sigh of relief when a guard closed the doors. The sudden quiet reminded her that the airport, though small, bustled.

She leaned back against the cushions and closed her eyes, hoping to avoid the entire world, especially Ray. She didn't want to be close to him, not emotionally, not physically, ever again. She prayed he wouldn't touch her. If he did, her resolve would crumble like stale, dry cake.

Even with her eyes tight shut, keeping her hands to herself, Cami was keenly aware of his presence. When he moved, she could hear the swish of his robes and the creak of the leather upholstery. His scent, which had always reminded her of exotic casbahs and romantic, foreign shores, seemed amplified here, on his native soil.

His nearness made every cell vibrate. The tiny hairs on her bare arms stood to attention. Her skin prickled. She hated what he could do to her so effortlessly.

She was thirsty, hungry, tired, grubby, exhausted. She wanted nothing more than a shower and her bed at home.

Something cool and hard touched her lips. "Drink," he said.

Opening her eyes, she saw a glass and obeyed, even though she didn't want anything from Ray. But fasting in protest would hurt no one but herself.

Orange juice, cool and sweet. "It isn't as good as back in Texas," she managed to croak.

"Of course it is not. The juice I gave you at my home had been freshly squeezed from my trees. This is some commercial product."

"Is it Adnani?"

"Yes. We grow citrus in a fertile region between the sea and the mountains. Beyond them, there is desert." He rolled down the window. Heat blasted into the car's interior. Ignoring it, he pointed outside at one of the banners decorating the limo. "See you our flag? The colors represent our country. Blue for sea and sky. The greenbelt. The golden desert sands."

"Wonderful." She didn't bother to keep the sourness out of her voice. However exotic and interesting this place might be, she didn't want to be in Adnan, and she swore that she wouldn't cooperate. After draining the glass of juice, she again closed her eyes, deliberately shutting Ray out.

"Cami, please. There is much you need to know. Your position—"

"Listen, Ray." She jerked upright and shot him a nasty glare. "There's something *you* need to know. Our marriage is over. I filed for divorce. I have no position here." She again turned away from him, curling her body into a corner of the limo.

The car remained quiet for the space of a few moments. She could hear only his even breathing.

"I am sorry," he said finally. "But I cannot grant you a divorce. My country is very unstable—"

"Grant me a divorce? What are you talking about?" Arrogant, too, as well as a snake. "Under Texas law, I have an absolute right to a divorce."

"We are not in Texas."

His quietly spoken words crashed down on her like an avalanche. *We are not in Texas.* The realities of her situation struck her. She was alone in a strange land, the captive wife of one of its princes. She had no pocketbook, no identification, no passport and no money.

She had nothing.

She *was* nothing.

The only thing she had was a husband she loathed. She was only someone's nameless, faceless wife.

Cami buried her face in her hands and tried not to cry from her despair and frustration.

"Camille, stop this silliness. This is no time to indulge in childish tantrums. You knew what you were taking on when we married. You knew I was a prince of Adnan—"

She jerked upright. "We never talked about it! I thought we'd live in Texas."

"I am not sure where we will live now. Much is happening here that you do not know about."

"I don't care to know." She turned away from him.

"You must. You are now Camille al-Rashad, the consort of a prince of Adnan, and that means responsibility. You are no longer pampered Cami Ellison."

Cami flinched. She scooted across the seat toward the open window, focusing on her surroundings instead of his hurtful, stinging words.

The limo was traveling through a busy part of the city. A business district, she supposed, based on the office buildings lining the streets. The wide boulevard was crowded with various kinds of transportation, from mules, bicycles and scooters, on up to Rolls-Royces. Billboards, many advertising the same products as in America, caught her eye. Most featured darkly handsome males with petite, dainty girls Cami figured were typical of Adnan.

The sidewalks were jammed; pedestrians of every age and race wore all manner of clothing.

Involuntarily fascinated, she said, "I see a lot of people in Western dress, including women. But I've heard that the Arab countries can be very repressive, especially toward females."

"Not Adnan. We were colonized by the French, you see, and are close to Europe. The European influence is very strong, especially in the cities and along the seacoast. Women need not wear the *abaya* or the veil, unless they choose.''

Cami frowned. ''Why would anyone want to go around wearing a black bedsheet?''

''The *abaya* is said to be very comfortable, though I would not know from experience. In the heat, the loose, thin fabrics are cool.''

''Black is hot in the sun.''

''In Adnan, the colors are different. See?'' Leaning closer to her, he pointed out the window. ''Young, unmarried women are in white to signify their innocence. Those in mourning may wear black; the long-widowed, gray. And married women choose any color they please, but the colors of our flag are the most popular.''

His nearness bothered her, grating against her already raw nerves. ''What about divorced women? What color do they wear?''

He yanked away. ''There are no divorced women in Adnan. Adnani understand the concepts of commitment and loyalty.'' He glowered at her, eyes smoldering.

She got right in his face. ''What about honesty, huh? Love?''

''I have never lied to you!''

''There are lies of omission, aren't there?'' He was evading her question. This time she wouldn't let him get away with it. ''And what about love?''

He snorted. ''Love. What is it about love? You Americans are obsessed with love. I am a prince of Adnan! Princes do not wed for love. I married you because you are beautiful, smart and wealthy. Plus, you were a virgin.''

''Not anymore.'' Bitter bile flooded her mouth. She'd saved herself for marriage only to discover she'd been a pawn in her deceitful husband's game of revenge.

''No.'' A smug smile spread across his face.

She longed to smack it away, but kept her hands to herself. The fleeting satisfaction she'd get from slapping him wasn't worth death by beheading.

The limo approached a large, elaborately decorated building. Surrounded by minarets and clad in mosaics, it glittered in the sun. Ahead of the car, a dark archway loomed.

She gulped and pointed out the window. ''Is that where I lose my head?''

Ray chuckled. ''It is true that the penalty for assaulting a royal is death, but you are my consort. You are exempt.''

''You could have said so before,'' Cami grumbled. The limo slid into the cool shadows beneath the arch.

''Please do not pretend you have been trembling in fear during this ride.''

The limo stopped in the middle of a cobbled square beside a multitude of other vehicles, including a silver Rolls Royce and a Humvee painted in camouflage colors. ''Who drives the Humvee?'' she asked.

''My brother, Tariq, the marshal of the military. He has always been pretentious.''

She remembered she loved to tease Ray. ''I think it's cool.''

"Cool. Ha." He snorted. "The grand vizier, my brother Sharif, prefers the Rolls."

"What does the king drive?"

"Kadar does not drive. He uses this limo or flies in the jet that brought you to Adnan."

She gave him a wry smile. "He'll probably find it somewhat the worse for wear."

"Why?" The chauffeur opened his door, and Ray exited, holding out his hand for Cami.

She took it. "The stuff they put in my coffee made me awfully sick."

His dark eyebrows drew together into a straight, black bar. "Is that so?" He dragged her out of the car and down a colonnade, hauling her through the parking lot and down another corridor.

She had to run to keep up with Ray's angry strides. "Well, yeah. You know I don't travel well." As they hurried through the palace, she caught bewildering glimpses of bustling offices and beautifully furnished living chambers with quiet servants arranging bouquets or polishing furniture.

"Hmmf." He urged her into a courtyard. Lush with tropical plants, it surrounded a central fountain.

Ray shoved open an elaborately carved door and immediately began shouting in Arabic to a man seated behind a large, dark wooden desk. The man, who wore white robes like Ray's, stood, yelling back. Soon the two were toe-to-toe in the middle of the room, leaving Cami, dumbfounded, by the door.

She sensed a presence behind her. She turned to see a small figure, clad in a dove-gray *abaya* with intricate embroidered trim, standing in the archway. The little lady reached up and drew back the hood of her garment, exposing dark hair streaked with silver. She smiled, her round, amber-skinned face wrinkling pleasantly.

The lady's gentleness, palpable as a mother's touch, soothed Cami's ruffled temper.

"Do not be startled. They have always been so, like oil and water." The older lady's cultured, precise tones revealed that she must have been educated in England.

"Who? Why?"

"Two of my sons, Kadar and Rayhan."

"You're...you're Ray's mom?"

"Yes. You may call me Zedda, if you wish. Everyone else does."

"Th-thank you."

"You are Rayhan's wife, yes? He did not exaggerate."

"What did he say?"

Zedda ran a gentle finger along Cami's cheek. "He said his wife was as beautiful as the dawn, with a heart worthy of a hunting falcon. That one smile from her was brighter than a beach full of diamonds."

Embarrassed and confused by the effusive praise, Cami dropped her head to examine the toes of her sandals. "Oh. And why is Ray so mad?"

"As for their dispute, the king refused to accept your marriage to Rayhan, so he had you brought here."

"The king, not Ray?"

"I believe Rayhan was aware of your journey, but not the circumstances." Zedda nodded toward the arguing brothers. "That is why he is so distressed. He is angry over your mistreatment."

"Is that the king?" Cami eyed the arguing pair. Ray didn't seem to treat his monarch with much respect.

"Yes, Kadar is my eldest."

"Why doesn't the king approve of me?"

"He desires Rayhan to wed another."

A chill raced across Cami's skin. "Who? Why?"

"The daughter of the Sheikh al-Qamra. The People of the Moon have much influence over the desert tribes, which speak of revolt against our family's rule."

Cami's head spun. What had she gotten herself into? She was prepared to run a ranch in Texas, not meddle in Adnani politics.

Childish shrieks and giggles distracted Cami from her conversation with Zedda. A little girl, her legs furiously pumping beneath a froth of pink skirts, raced across the courtyard. She was pursued by a woman in flapping black robes. Both vanished through another archway.

Zedda smiled. "My granddaughter, Selima. Her name means peaceful."

Cami laughed.

"You are a most pleasant young woman. You will soon come to my rooms to take tea, yes?"

Cami didn't want to stay in Adnan long enough to

attend tea parties, but Zedda was so kind. "I, uh, thank you."

Ray broke off his discussion to return to her side. "Zedda." He bent to kiss the lady's wrinkly cheek.

"Rayhan, your wife is tired and in need of cosseting." Zedda produced a key from a hidden pocket in her robe. "Take her to purdah."

Purdah! The word reminded Cami of secret, locked harems. She had a vision of herself imprisoned, never to see home again.

Rayhan frowned. "I had thought the old seraglio unused."

"It is maintained for the relaxation and convenience of the female members of the royal family." Zedda handed Cami the key.

"I did not know," he said.

"You had no reason to know. I will inform the servants that only you and your wife may be admitted for the next two days."

Chapter Ten

The Queen's seraglio rivaled any spa Cami had visited. Room after room of creamy marble bathing pools, each heated to a different temperature, dazzled her eyes and her senses. Elaborate, beautiful mosaics adorned every surface, with the colors of the Adnani flag prominent. The fragrances of citrus and jasmine perfumed the sultry, humid air.

Servants had evidently prepared the purdah before they arrived. Fresh towels sat in stacks near every pool. Tables loaded with fruit, meats and drink waited in each of the rooms.

Ray walked ahead of Cami toward one of the pools and, showing no trace of shyness, stripped off his robes, dropping them to the tiles. Turning, he smiled at her and held out his hand. "Come."

She stood rooted to the spot. "Ray, I don't want to fool around with you."

"Why not? It has been a long time, and we are married."

She sighed and looked away from him. She knew if she feasted her eyes on his dark, virile body, her restraint, already shaky, would shatter. Nothing would be resolved, and she'd be right back where she'd started: snared in a marriage built on revenge, deceptions and misunderstandings. She didn't want that. "Ray, we have to talk."

"Very well." He sprawled onto one of the marble benches nearby. His unabashed nakedness reminded her of the last time she'd seen him nude: when they'd made love aboard the *Corsair*. Her blood sped through her veins. She couldn't erase the memory of how his beautiful body felt joined with hers.

Rayhan grinned at Cami, hoping his casual pose and expression would hide his fiercely beating heart. The next few days would be a turning point in his marriage, his life, possibly even in the history of his country.

Alas, he had few weapons at his disposal with which to win back his bride. The frail link he'd nurtured with their lovemaking had snapped at the first sign of strain between them.

He noticed Cami averting her eyes from his body. Good. He knew from their lusty honeymoon that he did not repel his wife. She'd also tried to keep her distance in the limo. All of this meant she was afraid she'd lose her determination if she came too close or even looked at him.

The best means of reclaiming her remained seduction. Cami's wild sexuality, which he'd awakened, made her his thrall. At the same time, he had to respect her intelligence, intuition and deeply held morality.

Her anger was powerful and righteous. The peculiar obsession of American girls for true love would hamper him. Unless he explained himself with utmost clarity, Cami was bound to resent and misunderstand his motivations.

"I need to know what's going on here," she said.

At last his foolish young wife was concerned with something beyond herself. "Much is at stake. The basis for it all is the fractured nature of Adnan. You see, my country is comprised of several tribes. Generally we get along well. Sometimes we don't. There are times when the interests of one tribe may conflict with those of another. The desert people may conflict with the hill people, who think differently than do the inhabitants of the cities along the seacoast. The concerns of the farmers are unlike the problems of those who fish in the sea."

"I see." Cami's blue gaze held an shrewd glint. "From what tribe are you?"

"The people of the cities, who have long been traders, merchants and financiers, sought to unify the country under the banner of their leaders. My family." Because the conversation had taken a serious turn, he donned his robes, but allowed them to gape open up top. When they'd made love, Cami had seemed fixated with his chest. He didn't know why, but that didn't matter.

"Traders?" Cami lifted her brows.

"Yes, well, some of us were what you might call

pirates.'' He shrugged. ''In the old days. But, since the end of World War II, we have provided the strong leadership Adnan needed lest one of the larger Arab nations swallow us.''

''Is that a danger?'' Her eyes widened.

''Yes. You may have read that there is much fundamentalist, anti-American unrest in our neighbor to the east. Most of us Adnani wish to remain separate from these problems, and to chart an independent course.''

''A pro-American course?''

''Yes. We believe that trade alliances with the United States and the European Union will greatly benefit our people. But many, especially the nomadic desert peoples, disagree. Your intransigence is perceived as an insult. To complicate matters, there is the situation of my engagement.''

She looked away. ''Your mother said that the king wanted you to marry someone else.''

''Yes.'' He waited a moment or two. ''I refused.''

''What's the problem?'' Cami asked, her eyes hard and cold as blue lapis. ''I filed for divorce. You're free if you choose.''

Rayhan swallowed against his dry throat. Rising, he stepped over to a table loaded with food, drink and sweetmeats. Tugged between three competing loves—his family, his country and his wife—his heart churned.

He gave her a bleak smile. ''Divorcing one wife to marry another is not freedom.''

She followed him. ''Wouldn't it make a lot of things easier?''

"Perhaps, but it was arranged by my family without my consent. I refuse to be a political pawn. Plus, there is the issue of the oil." He poured her a glass of fruit juice, then handed it to her.

"How's oil an issue? Except for the situation between you and my dad, oil's not an issue but a benefit." She sipped.

"Oil has only recently been found in Adnan. We lack the technology to exploit our resources. The king hesitates to ally with any of the other oil-producing nations. That is where you come in." Rayhan selected a bunch of delicate, pale green grapes.

"Me?"

"My family is aware of the source of your wealth. The fact is, your oil property automatically makes you and me the resident royal experts in the subject."

She narrowed her eyes. "As you might say, I refuse to be a political pawn."

He sighed. "I will admit to you there is a slender line between political participation and...pawnship. Is that a word?"

She laughed, which pleased him beyond reason. He'd placated his wife and put her in a good humor. Perhaps there was hope for their marriage.

"No," she said. "It's probably not a word, but I understand what you mean."

"Cami, you would have more power than most Adnani brides, even the princesses. My sisters' function has been to make advantageous marriages and to produce children. You will be more."

"Just as you have always wished to be more." Cami had never experienced such complex emotions, not even during the horrible moment when she realized that both her father and her husband had betrayed her trust.

While proud that Ray thought her capable of such responsibility, she still resented the fact that he'd married her for reasons other than love. Political advantage was now added to revenge and sex. Such motives objectified her and made a mockery of their marriage and her emotions.

Underlying it all was a deep fear that she wouldn't measure up.

"My wife, I have never forced you into anything and I never will. I give you my solemn promise that nothing will happen that you do not freely choose."

She stumbled to a bench and slumped onto it, covering her face with her hands. "I don't know what to do," she whispered through her fingers. "I never guessed any of this would happen. I'm not ready for this."

His warmth brushed her side as he sat next to her. "Why do you not see yourself as you are?"

She raised her head, studying his dark, serious face. "What do you mean?"

"The woman I married is intelligent, strong and capable. She has the courage of a pride of lions and the insight of a seer."

"I didn't know you thought of me so highly." Cami remembered that Ray's mother had mentioned that he'd lavishly complimented her.

"I see you as you are. Cami, I may not choose to make romantic love the basis for marriage, but I do believe in respect." He placed the uneaten grapes onto a platter, then took both her hands in his. "I married you. I intend for you to be the mother of our children. Does that not mean anything to you?"

"It means a lot, I guess, but—"

"You need decide nothing at this moment. Why do you not take my mother's advice? Enjoy this place."

He reached for her clothing, tugging on it.

"Ray, please." She drew back and took off her dress without his help.

His dark eyes narrowed. "The implication that I would need to force you is an insult."

She felt her flush all the way to the soles of her feet. "I didn't mean—"

"No matter." He gestured with one hand, as if he didn't care, but she knew better. She'd seen the hurt in his eyes, and hated herself for it. Though he might be a snake and a skunk, her husband wasn't a rapist.

His dark gaze surveyed her.

She shivered under his thorough scrutiny. "Quit looking at me like that!"

"Like what?"

"A bug under a microscope."

"I am ever fascinated by your body. Though I do wonder whether even a scrap of food has passed your lips since I left Texas." His fingers descended the ladder of her rib cage, forcing her to recall past, happier times.

Shoving away the memories, she stood to avoid his hands, his glance. "I haven't felt much like eating lately."

"We will fatten you up here. You'll be nice and

round, like an Adnani girl. Now join me.'' He took two quick steps and dove into the pool.

Shining drops sprayed in a silvery arc through the air, splashing her panties. She pulled them off, kicked away her sandals, then slipped into the water.

Ray had picked a pool heated to just above blood temperature, and it felt like paradise against her skin.

Closing her eyes, Cami let herself relax.

After bathing and eating, Ray led Cami to a bedroom. Without looking around, she fell onto the mattress and slept like a hibernating bear.

Awakening disoriented, she stared through the warm darkness. From an archway to her right, shafts of moonlight slashed into the room. Where was she?

Her husband warmed the bed by her side, and for a brief moment, she was comforted by his presence. Then reality crashed down on her. Her father's sins, Ray's betrayal and her own stupidity had combined in a horrible, overwhelming vortex.

Crushed by the rubble of her trashed life, Cami clutched a pillow to her chest. She moaned at the smothering weight of her despair. The sobs choking her throat escaped.

Ray's arms wrapped around her, cuddling her close. She pushed him away as best she could. Too weak to move his rock-solid body very far, she instead found herself caressing his chest. She jerked away.

"Let me touch you. Let me help."

The raw need in his voice battered her weakened

defenses. "No, please," she managed to whisper. "I have to work this out alone."

He didn't let go of her. "No, you do not. I am your husband. You will work things out with me."

"Oh, Ray. Don't you realize you're the problem?"

"My darling wife. Did you think we would have no difficulties in our marriage?" Holding her tight, he kissed away her tears.

"Huh." Jolted, Cami realized that Ray had made a good point. She blinked.

"I married you for a lifetime. Of course there will be some bumps in the road."

"This is more than a little bump in the road."

"I realize I must struggle to prove myself worthy of you." He kissed her mouth with utmost gentleness.

Regardless of his tender caress, she let her anger shield her pain, blocking the hurt away, even from herself. Gradually she calmed enough to resist Ray when he nibbled at her lower lip.

"No, please."

"Why not?"

"It's wrong."

"How can this be wrong?" He caressed her breast, fingering the nipple. It rose, tender and aroused. "We are married."

"We married for the wrong reasons. You don't love me." She hated saying those words, hated admitting to herself she was a failure as a woman. The knowledge that her husband didn't love her sliced like a steel blade through her heart.

"So? And what of your feelings? You have said that you love me. Are your feelings of no account?"

Ray's contorted line of reasoning jarred Cami.

She still loved him. With a start she realized she'd married Ray because she loved him, and not because he loved her.

"But...but—"

"But what?" he asked. "I respect and esteem you. I am willing to care for you and our children forever."

She teared up again, using the sheet to dab at her eyes.

"You are distressed. Why will you not allow me to offer the comfort of my body? Would you not feel better?"

"B-because...because...I'm confused," she wailed. "I have so much and so little. I have everything but a husband who loves me."

"I understand that is very important to you. But what is love, Cami?"

"Don't you know? Oh, Ray!" This was worse. He didn't know what love was. How could he love anyone? He'd never be able to love her as she needed and deserved.

"Cami, I love you to the extent I am able. So, I love you. All right?"

Renewed anger flared. "No, it's not all right! You're lying."

"How can you say that? When have I ever lied to you? I'm not lying! Cami, you are making us both crazy." Ray sprang out of bed to pace up and down the room with jerky strides. "I am your husband. Whatever you need, I give. You need me to love you. So I love you! What is the problem?"

He was so over the top that the only thing she could do was utter a broken laugh.

"At least I have made you laugh," he grumbled, sitting on the bed beside her. "Rayhan, the buffoon."

"You're not a buffoon." She wiped her cheeks with the backs of her hands, then sighed.

He pulled her into his arms again. "Cami, you are exhausted. No more crying, eh? Now let's sleep."

Too tired to fight him off, she allowed him to cradle her in his arms until, at last, she slept.

Rayhan watched Cami rest, as he'd done during that most joyous of times, their honeymoon. A starwatcher, he needed little sleep. Normally he'd get out of bed and go to his minaret to stargaze, letting his imagination roam the galaxies. Here in Adnan, he'd again become a frequent visitor to the Royal Observatory, the place where he'd first learned to explore the heavens.

Tonight he preferred to watch his wife. As slumber put her tension to flight, he could see the tight muscles in her face loosen. The natural, sweet curve of her lips returned.

Rayhan took hope from that serene smile, believing it meant that deep down, in her soul, Cami was happy with their marriage. Could she look so calm in her sleep if she were truly distressed?

Despite her crazy fixation with love, he had to win her. Everything he cared about was at stake—most importantly, Cami's happiness and that of the family he craved.

When Cami awakened, she was alone in a big bed. Taking stock of her surroundings, she realized she was in someone's sumptuous living quarters. A stack of books on the chest of drawers included volumes in English, French and Arabic.

Ray's room in the palace, she figured. The massive bed bore her husband's scent beside her on the dented pillow. He'd slept with her, had held and comforted her. She appreciated that. Yesterday had left her drained.

As always, Ray had been gentle and kind. At the same time, she noticed changes in her husband since she'd arrived in Adnan. He seemed more open and emotional; she remembered what he'd told his mother about her. And he'd been incensed with his brother, the king, at her treatment.

Drawing in a calming breath, Cami realized her fury at Ray had retreated, leaving an open, bloody wound. She wanted her anger back. It had shielded her against this pain.

The two people she trusted most in the world had deceived her, and she'd been clueless. How could she ever depend upon anyone again? Why should she? And how could she trust her own judgment in the future?

Cami rubbed a fist over her chest, as though she could massage her heartache away.

She had to cling to her love, believing in the truth her heart told.

But should she settle for a one-sided sham of a marriage?

She sighed and stretched, then noticed a pile of blue fabric trimmed with gold embroidery lying across the foot of the bed. Cami got up to check it out and found clothing like the hooded garment Zedda wore. When in Rome, Cami thought.

After tossing the simple robe over her head, she left their room and went outside to a colonnaded courtyard. It rimmed lush gardens, radiating familar Adnani aromas of citrus and jasmine. The tinkle of a fountain met her ears. Squinting upward, she guessed that the clear, golden light signaled midmorning, as it lacked the intensity of noon or the colors of sunset.

Good heavens. She'd slept more than eighteen hours. Whatever the king's agents had put in the coffee had packed quite a wallop.

At the far end of the courtyard, Cami saw Zedda seated at a round table, pouring something for two little girls. One of them looked like Selima, the active toddler Cami had seen the day before.

She advanced on the tea party with hesitant steps, unsure of her welcome.

Zedda looked up as Cami approached. "Look, children! Here is Auntie Cami, Uncle Rayhan's new wife. She is from America." Zedda enunciated very clearly. "We must speak only English so she can understand us."

"Thank you." Cami walked toward the only empty chair at the table.

"Please, sit." Zedda gestured. "You saw Selima yesterday, yes? And this is Sadira, our little star. They are my daughter Leila's children."

Both girls were neatly clad in pinafore-style dresses with sailor collars. They wore white gloves on their tiny hands, which they carefully removed to eat the delicate cucumber sandwiches and drink steaming mint tea.

Cami was enchanted. For reasons known only to her, Zedda had recreated an English tea party in the midst of this wildly exotic locale. The little girls co-operated wholeheartedly, sticking out their pinkie fingers to sip the tea. They politely chatted about *Alice in Wonderland* and *Peter Pan,* which Cami gathered was their most recent bedtime reading.

She happily joined in, spreading the lace napkin across her lap and pouring tea out of the china pot for Zedda. Soon, however, the girls' nannies came to retrieve the children.

"Did you enjoy my granddaughters?" Zedda asked, sipping her tea.

"Yes, I did. A lot more than I expected." Passing a hand over her stomach, Cami wondered about her own condition.

"You are not enceinte, my dear. I would know if you were."

Cami's heart clenched. "How did you know what I was thinking? And why are you sure I'm not pregnant? I've had a lot of the symptoms."

Zedda shrugged. "It does not take a genius to discern what a young wife is thinking about when she touches her stomach while discussing children. As for your condition, I have seven children and four grandchildren, and expect that number to increase. You are not pregnant. If you have suffered symptoms—the morning illness and so forth—that is due to the stress between you and Rayhan."

Cami sighed, setting down her cup. "Zedda, I don't know what to do."

"Do you wish to talk about it? If you do not want me to repeat the conversation to my son, I will keep it a secret."

"Thanks, but it doesn't matter. He knows why I'm upset. See, he doesn't love me, and he married me for all the wrong reasons." Cami explained the situation with the land, the oil and her father.

"Hmm." Zedda fingered her napkin, a thoughtful expression on her face. "That explains much."

"What?"

"Rayhan left about ten years ago, after quarreling with his father—my husband. My son told me at the time that he needed to prove himself to Malik. But Rayhan stayed away for years, until his father had died. I now understand why he did not return. When he failed to make a quick killing in oil, he could not face Malik until honor was satisfied."

"And now it is, by his marriage to me."

"Yes. Malik would not have respected Rayhan had he returned dishonored. My husband was a strong man, Cami, but not a particularly loving one. We married for political advantage, to unify the country."

"That seems to be the tendency around here." She felt her jaw tighten.

"Yes, it is. I know it is foreign to you, but it is not uncommon, even in the West."

"I've read that boys learn how to be men from their fathers."

"That is not necessarily the case. Rayhan is nothing like his father, I assure you. Perhaps Rayhan married you for the wrong reasons, Cami, but perhaps the two of you will stay together because of the right ones.''

Chapter Eleven

"**M**y wife." Ray's warm hand massaged Cami's shoulder. She'd been so engrossed in conversation that she hadn't noticed Ray until he'd touched her.

Turning, she scrutinized him with fresh eyes. Eyes that looked beyond the facade to the rejected youth beneath. Eyes that saw the man caught between two cultures, struggling to do the right thing by both.

"Hello, Ray." Cami caught his hand and rubbed it against her cheek.

His eyes widened, but he didn't appear displeased. "Cami, I would ask that you join our meeting. This morning, we discuss oil, your expertise."

Cami rose and circled the table to Zedda's side. Leaning over, she hugged the older woman. "Thank you so much."

Zedda stroked Cami's cheek. "You are most welcome, my daughter. Go now, until the evening meal."

As they walked together down the colonnade, Ray

said to Cami, "I am glad to see you close to my mother."

"She's a dear person."

"Perhaps you need a mother to confide in."

"Maybe. Talking with her sure went a long way to making me feel better."

Ray came to a heavily carved door. Stopping, he faced Cami. "Whatever happens now, do not be intimidated."

"I don't understand why they want to talk to me. I'm only nineteen!"

"You have been studying the oil business for years, have you not?"

"Ye-es, but—"

"Cami, listen. Oil was only recently discovered in Adnan. Few Adnani knows anything about this matter, and my brothers, especially Tariq, do not trust outsiders."

"But what am I?"

"You're family." He touched her shoulder, and even that fleeting caress was enough to distract her.

With a deep breath Cami reclaimed her focus. "I'm an American, and a woman to boot."

"We are not like other Arab cultures. Adnan was heavily influenced by the Europeans. My brothers will listen to you, just as they will consult and listen to others. They may not agree with you, but they will listen."

"But—"

"Hush." He placed a finger over her lips, and she resisted kissing it. "No more buts. You are the consort of a prince of Adnan. Remember who you are."

He pushed open the door, revealing an enormous room dominated by a big, round table.

Cami entered, heart pounding. Inside, the only person Cami recognized was the king. Ray introduced a dark man dressed in camouflage fatigues as Tariq ibn-Malik al-Rashad. She recalled that Ray's brother Tariq ran the Adnani military. Brother Sharif, also present, was the grand vizier, which she understood as equivalent to a prime minister.

An older man in dark robes, who wore a disapproving frown, was introduced as Uncle Hamid, the local mullah. He was a religious leader, she supposed. He didn't speak to her, but said something in Arabic to the King.

Kadar responded, his voice silken, "We speak in English as a courtesy to our guest, the consort of Rayhan, Prince of Adnan."

"She does not bow properly," Uncle Hamid observed, in heavily accented English.

"I'm an American, sir. We don't bow at all." Cami stared into his dark brown eyes.

Hamid sniffed and elevated his hawk nose. "How can this young woman advise us?"

Ray escorted Cami to a chair opposite the males, then sat beside her. "My wife owns and manages several thousand acres of oil property in Texas. She knows more about the oil business than anyone else in this room."

That shut Uncle Hamid up. Cami lifted her chin and looked around the table, catching each man's gaze in turn. "How can I help you out?"

The king leaned forward. "We recently received a

proposal from the OPEC to provide equipment and personnel to develop Adnani oil.''

Cami narrowed her eyes, remembering. The previous day, Ray had mentioned that the king hesitated to ally with OPEC. ''What is the price of their assistance?'' she asked.

''A percentage of the oil extracted,'' Sharif said.

''For how long?''

Her question was met by silence.

''Would training of Adnani personnel be included? Would the equipment become Adnani after a suitable period of time, say five years?'' she wanted to know.

''Those are excellent topics for negotiation.'' Sharif lounged back in his chair, eyes sparkling.

''And what about intangible costs?'' Cami ran her fingers along the carved edge of the table. ''Many OPEC nations have political agendas. Does Adnan share their concerns?''

Tariq pounded on the table with his fist. ''Exactly my point! We cannot afford to draw closer to extremists. And yet they are sure to seek our involvement in their disputes.''

''I'd negotiate a lease-purchase contract with a neutral country, or even a private concern,'' Cami said.

''And we must make certain that they train Adnani citizens to run our facilities.'' Ray finally spoke up, and she was grateful for his support. ''We cannot be dependent upon outsiders.''

''Yes!'' The king spoke. ''Rayhan, will you and your consort join us tomorrow for further discussions? You will conduct the negotiations, will you not?''

''I will, but today I belong to my wife.''

The king gestured. "Go now, but tomorrow we consult with the Royal Dutch Petroleum Company."

After inclining his head in acknowledgment, Ray led Cami from the room.

"You greatly impressed my brothers," Ray told Cami as he escorted her out of the palace.

She shrugged. "I just said what they wanted to hear."

"Very diplomatic. Perhaps they'll forgive me for marrying you."

"Are they really upset with you about that?" She pulled the blue hood of her garment over her head to avoid the intense noon sun.

"Yes, but today you have greatly swayed them, I think. Oh, the old-fashioned, like Uncle Hamid, will never approve of you, but he doesn't approve of anything. He's never liked me." Holding her arm, Ray expertly negotiated a sidewalk crowded with pedestrians, bicycles and scooters. He ducked through an archway, hauling her with him.

Abruptly the atmosphere seemed to change. Away from the road, with its noisy motorized vehicles, this area radiated a sense of the mysterious and the exotic.

A shop hung with thick, richly stitched carpets crowded the walkway to Cami's left. On her right, several men jammed a table, drinking aromatic, cinnamon-scented coffee out of tiny cups while volubly arguing in Arabic. Nearby, two silent men in striped robes bent over a chessboard, their faces serious.

The cobbles of the uneven street underfoot pressed

through the thin soles of Cami's sandals. "Where are we?" she asked.

"The old souk." Ray grinned at her. "I thought you might want to see more of my country while you decide about our marriage."

"Would we live in Adnan, at the palace?"

"Part of the time, I should think." He shouldered his way through the crowd.

She and Ray spent a relaxed, friendly afternoon wandering the narrow streets of old Syed. Cami shopped for clothes and accessories, choosing additional Adnani robes to wear.

She also bought loose, flowing outfits consisting of calf-length tunics and matching pants, with a *shayla,* a head scarf, to complete the look. Rather than haul parcels around, they arranged to have them delivered to the palace.

Ray paid for everything, showing her the curious little Adnani coins and colorful bills. A copper *birr* was roughly equivalent to a penny; *cedi* were like dimes. The major form of currency was the *dinar,* and twelve *dinarii* were equivalent to one American dollar.

"I wonder where my pocketbook is," Cami said.

"Those *hayawat* didn't think to grab your handbag?" Ray snorted. "Kadar shouldn't have sent fools to America who don't know the customs."

"We'll have to phone to cancel my credit cards."

"A nuisance. If I had known how clumsy Kadar's operatives would have been..." Ray shook his head. "I am sorry. It should not have happened."

"Yeah, and I need to call home so my father

doesn't worry. Don't you want to know how he's doing?'' Cami didn't keep annoyance out of her tone. Ray had put her father in the hospital and hadn't bothered to inquire about him.

He grinned at her as he led her past a coppersmith's stall, hung with shiny, hammered metal pans and bowls. "Why do you think I do not know the state of his health?''

She stopped to stare at him. "Do you?''

"Of course. Your father and I have spoken frequently since you moved to San Antonio.''

"You have?''

"Yes, and why not? We have had our differences, yes, but we are united in our concern for you.''

"Huh.'' Cami stared at him, flabbergasted.

He threw up his hands. "All right, all right, I admit it. I apologized to him.''

Stopping short in the middle of the walkway, she ignored the throngs of tourists and shoppers who were forced to sidestep them. "You apologized to him! But he swindled you! And what about me?''

"One question at a time, please.'' Taking her arm, he urged her to an empty table at an outdoor restaurant. "Yes, he cheated me, but I was wrong.''

A waiter arrived, and Ray, speaking in Arabic, ordered something. Cami sat, startled beyond measure by what Ray had said.

He'd realized he was wrong and without prompting from her or anyone, had independently called to apologize to her father. "What did Dad say?''

Ray shrugged. "He seemed surprised, but not as surprised as are you. And he also apologized. He explained that, ten years ago, his business had taken a downturn and he had trouble putting food on the table for you. He needed the cash I offered.''

''But it wasn't fair to you.''

''Time heals much. I love the Double Eagle. My beautiful Arabians are prized all over the world.''

''Then why did you pursue your revenge?''

''I was a fool, and very wrong. I did not realize how wrong I was until I saw what my vendetta did to you, my wife.''

She flushed, and her anger returned. ''Yeah, too bad your victim wasn't my father.''

He shrugged. ''I took that which was most precious to him. But I do not regret what I did. I value you at least as much as does he.''

''I won't be treated as though I'm...I'm a piece of pr-property.'' She stood, bumping into the server, who bore an enameled brass tray with two coffees, which spilled. ''Oh, I'm sorry.''

Cami sat back down into the uncomfortable metal patio chair while the waiter, babbling in Arabic, cleaned up the mess.

''Your anger cloaks your love for me,'' Ray said. ''Can you not admit it?''

Biting her lip, she turned her head. A teenager on a scooter, with tiny headphones anchored in his ears and a Walkman clipped to the belt of his jeans, zipped by.

''Cami, look at me. I need you. We are wed. Can you let go of your anger? For us? For our marriage?''

With difficulty she faced him.

He sat regarding her, worry in his eyes. ''You are

thin. You haven't eaten much since we separated. Can you forgive me, for yourself?'' He reached across the table and took her hand in his, rubbing a finger on her wedding band.

She saw that he still wore his ring, and her heart split in two. Misery welled up in that empty, broken place. ''Oh, Ray, I'm so hurt and mad. When I drop the wall of that rage, I'm…destroyed. How could you? Why?''

''At first, it was the revenge.'' His voice softened. ''Then it became something else.''

''What?''

''I wanted you. I still do. Is that so hard to believe?''

''Yes.'' She bent her head and fiddled with her braid.

''You are the most insecure girl.'' He leaned over the table. ''It was certainly not the money, Cami. My mother had given me a large cash gift to set myself up in your country. Though the transaction drained my savings, part of the problem was the shame of being outwitted.''

''None of that was my fault.''

''You are right, and I was wrong. Having you is more important than revenge.''

''Well, that's nice to hear.'' Cami met her husband's gaze squarely, and he didn't flinch away. Perhaps he's telling the truth, she thought. Perhaps there's some hope for this marriage, after all. ''What did my dad say when your brother had me abducted?''

"He wasn't happy about it, so when we return to the palace perhaps you will phone him."

She bit her lip. "I should have thought of that before."

"Cami, do not blame yourself. You were exhausted when you arrived. I have already talked with Charles this day, before you awakened."

Shouting drew Cami's attention away from their conversation. Voices gabbling in English, French and Arabic assailed her ears.

Ray said something in Arabic she couldn't understand, but sounded vaguely irritable, followed by, "Here they come."

"Glad you switched to English, but what are you talking about?"

"Reporters." His eyelid twitched.

"What?"

He scratched his temple. "I am a prince, and our situation has caught the media's attention. Worse, someone leaked information on your divorce suit to the press. That has caused some anti-American feeling."

"Oh, my God. I didn't realize my personal life would cause an international incident."

A woman dressed in a navy, Western-style suit stood near Cami's chair, snapping orders in Arabic. A cameraman pointed his machine at Cami and Ray.

Speaking into a microphone, the woman said, "This is Lasca bint Wasim, reporting from the souk in old Syed, for the Adnan English Language Network. We have tracked down Prince Rayhan and his controversial American consort, Camille Ellison, in

the old souk. Are you enjoying our city, madame?''
She thrust a microphone in Cami's face.

''Ah, uh, yeah, very much.'' Cami's mind froze,
and she couldn't help sounding like a dork. She really
wasn't up for this princess stuff.

''Have you given up your attempt to divorce Prince
Rayhan in the Texas courts?''

Though Cami's brains might have taken a vacation,
her temper hadn't. But before she could say something unwise, she recalled something Ray had told
her. ''Remember who you are.''

Who was she? At age nineteen, Cami didn't really
know, but she was sure of one thing: she wasn't
someone who blabbed about her private life. ''I'm
sorry, but I can't comment about that.'' Pulling at the
front of her hood, she tugged it over her face, retreat-
ing into its protection.

To her immense relief, the reporter immediately
withdrew, turning to the camera to finish her story.
''As you can see, Prince Rayhan's consort has
adopted the traditional garb of our country as well as
the usual response of the royal women to questions
from the press: no comment. This has been an on-
the-spot report from Syed City. Back to you, Jamal.''
The media and their cameras packed up their equipment, then left as quickly as they'd arrived.

Cami turned to Ray. ''Is this going to happen often?''

He smiled. ''I hope not. This is the first time the
press has paid a great deal of attention to me. They
are usually much more concerned with my brothers.
And, as you can imagine, my mother is a favorite.''

"The reporter seemed aggressive, yet respectful."

"Yes, Lasca is one of the best of the new breed of Adnani professional women. She maintains respect for our customs while pursuing her career. She knows she won't get anything out of us if she pushes too hard."

The event troubled Cami. What kind of life would she lead in Adnan, especially if she became involved with politics?

"By the way, you did very well. That Lasca compared you to the other princesses will help to undercut those who disapprove of our marriage."

"The whole thing is sorta...weird."

He shrugged. "Yes, it is a new life for you. But it is interesting, is it not?"

She laughed, realizing that nothing bad had actually happened. "Maybe I can handle the consort thing."

"There is no maybe about it. You are perfect."

Glowing with his praise, Cami found herself in charity with her husband for the rest of the day. They returned to the palace in the afternoon to rest before the evening meal.

The sound of the shower awakened her at dusk. She stretched, then followed Ray and bathed. For the evening she selected one of the new outfits she'd purchased, a pant set with a matching scarf. Then she piled her hair on top of her head with beautiful enameled combs she'd bought that day in the souk.

She pirouetted in front of the mirror in Ray's room. She loved her new tunic and pants. In a heavy cream silk with gold and green embroidery, it flowed like water against her skin. "I feel like an exotic desert princess," she said, chuckling.

"You *are* an exotic desert princess, my wife."

"We're dressed like twins." She grinned at him. He stood behind Cami and she regarded them both in the mirror.

Ray, who had selected a pale *thobe* with narrow green stripes, arranged her outfit's matching scarf around her throat.

"Not over the head?" she asked.

"I am glad you are willing to attempt our customs, especially since Western women often find them confining. But no, not at home," he said. "In the Arab culture, there is a distinct difference between the public and the private. You need not cover your head or face in the palace."

"All right." Cami knotted the scarf around her neck.

"I wonder who we will see tonight."

"The family, I presume?"

"Yes, and possibly guests, of a political nature. We entertain often."

"Will your brothers be there?"

"Perhaps, though Tariq often is away, inspecting troops or on maneuvers. Habiba, the queen, is in her ninth month of pregnancy, and she frequently takes meals in her rooms. If so, Kadar may attend her."

"I haven't met her." Cami loosened the oblong scarf and tried draping it over her elbows.

"She is a lovely person, my sister Habiba, but we greatly fear for her life. She is not—how would you say it?—she is not a good breeder."

"How many children do she and the king have?"

"None, I am afraid. She has had, alas, several miscarriages. There is no crown prince yet."

"That's not good."

"Adnani law would permit Kadar to take another wife, but he refuses to do so."

"He can have two wives?"

"All the royals can. It is the means by which the succession is secured." Her husband's voice was bland, neutral. His hooded gaze revealed nothing.

Cami swallowed past a frightened lump in her throat. What if Ray decided to... No. She couldn't. No way. Never.

She went to the door, turned and waited, giving Ray the chance to deny any plan to take another wife.

The room remained quiet.

Then she said, "Is that what you want?"

He hesitated. "I am experiencing considerable pressure from my brothers in regard to the Princess al-Qamra."

Her temper flared. Those rats had the gall to hit her up for advice while sabotaging her relationship with her husband.

But did she really want this marriage? Her innards roiled, matching her confusion.

One thing was clear. She wouldn't share Ray. "If that's what it'll take to fit in here, forget it."

His jaw worked. "I beg your pardon?"

"You heard what I said." She sucked in a deep breath, fighting the hot tears springing to her eyes. "I'll take the next plane home tomorrow morning."

Jerking open the heavy wood door, she left him.

She wanted to slam the door behind her, but controlled herself. Instead, she closed the door with a quiet click. Slamming the door would be immature. She'd learned better.

On shaky feet, Cami stepped onto the tiled colonnade surrounding the palace's inner courtyard. Evening had fallen. Despite her inner turmoil, the scent of flowers and the sounds of the fountain soothed her. Shrieking and running, small children played tag along the dimly lit pathways; Cami was sure she saw Selima pushing a small, serious-faced boy, teasing him into play.

At the far end of the courtyard, she could see Ray's brothers filling their plates at a long buffet. At a round table nearby, Zedda sat with one of the little girls, feeding her.

She couldn't face others yet and wasn't very hungry, anyway. Wrapping the *shayla* over her head to conceal her face, she wandered through the dusk until she found a quiet bench by a fountain.

Trailing a hand in the water, she prayed for calm and peace. However, she'd meant what she'd said. She didn't know how, but she had to make her way home to Texas in the morning.

Even though she adored Ray with all her heart, she couldn't stomach a rival for her husband's love.

Chapter Twelve

As he left their room, Rayhan wondered what the night would bring. Until he'd said exactly the wrong words, he'd cherished hopes that his marriage would move back onto the pleasurable course it had traveled during their honeymoon. But Omar Khayyam had said, "the moving finger writes, and having writ, moves on."

Rayhan couldn't undo the damage, made worse by his inability to express himself in English to his wife. His command of the language had faltered since he'd returned to his homeland. Now he spoke and even thought in Arabic.

He'd been struck dumb by Cami's assumption that he'd take another wife. With her sturdy notions of morality, she would never accept multiple marriage. But the al-Qamra should be brought into the royal family, for the good of Adnan.

But why did he have to be the sacrificial lamb?

He'd wanted a place in the political life of his country, but the price was too high.

He heard the clatter of Cami's heels on the tiled pavement, somewhere within the now-dark gardens. About to go to her side, he heard a familiar voice hail her.

"Young woman!"

Uncle Hamid, speaking to his wife, alone? Rayhan's fists clenched. The customs of their country limited unchaperoned contact between men and women. Why was the tradition-bound old mullah accosting his wife? And what would Cami do and say? She wasn't aware of local customs.

"Young woman!"

"Excuse me?" Cami sounded puzzled. "Hi, uh, sir."

Rayhan grinned. She wasn't sure how to address Uncle Hamid.

"It would be best for you to go back to America. The Princess al-Qamra, she should marry Prince Rayhan."

"You better clear that with Prince Rayhan." Cami's voice remained calm.

"The People of the Moon are powerful family in Adnan. They can make it werry uncomfable for the al-Rashads."

"Maybe."

"You seek to deal with me? I deal. I offer you ten thousand dinarii to give back Prince Rayhan's ring."

"Ten thousand dinarii?" To anyone but Rayhan, Cami would sound as though she was considering his uncle's offer. Cami continued, "Ten thousand dinarii? I'm not very good at math. What's that, a little over eight hundred dollars American?''

Rayhan nearly laughed out loud. Cami had probably spent more than that on his wedding gift. He knew his wife; the size of the offer wouldn't matter, even if it were ten million dinarii and she were poor as a desert rat. Though she might harbor doubts about their marriage, Cami couldn't be bought. She loved him.

He knew his wife, but did she know her husband? Rayhan, thunderstruck by the turn his thoughts had taken, considered the situation from a new perspective. Did not his Camille deserve the same confidence he enjoyed?

Rayhan put his personal concerns aside when his uncle again spoke.

''That is not enough? You are a greedy creature, even for an American woman. Twenty thousand!''

''But he's a prince.'' Cami chuckled. ''What if I want to be a princess?''

''We are royals, too. So I give you my son. He is a good boy. Twenty-five thousand!''

Cami's giggles increased to unladylike whoops. Rayhan could hear her heels erratically scraping the pavement as she staggered away from the old mullah.

She came into his view, clutching her sides, tears of merriment leaking from the corners of her eyes. He caught her before she tripped over her high heels, carefully lowering her to a bench.

''Did you hear that?'' Sucking in a breath, Cami visibly tried to control herself. ''That old skunk tried to bribe me!''

"I heard."

"Aren't you upset? You're only worth a measly two grand!"

"You are forgetting that he also offered his son."

"Oh, that's right." She turned to him, her eyes brimming with mirth. "Maybe I should meet this guy and give this some thought—"

"Maybe you should remember you'd have to put up with the, er, old skunk." Taking her hand, he led her to the buffet tables.

Cami sniffed the enticing aromas of saffron, cumin and cinnamon. She found a variety of Adnani dishes, including her now-beloved b'stila pie, as well as American and European favorites. She opted for the local food, selecting couscous with stewed lamb and roasted vegetables.

Ray guided her to a table occupied by the king, their brother Sharif, and Zedda, who dandled Sadira on her knee. Cami sat and sipped the mint tea Zedda poured for her. She noticed that some of the Adnani used forks, while others ate with their right hands, allowing servants to frequently rinse and dry their fingers.

If not for the colorful clothing and Adnani style of eating, the scene could be any family at dinner.

Despite the laughter they'd just shared, nothing had changed. Until Rayhan gave her his love without qualification, she'd never be anything but an appendage…possibly even just the number two wife. She'd bluffed Uncle Hamid only because she refused to let him force her hand. She'd make her own decisions, in her own time.

She'd still return to Texas in the morning. She didn't know quite how, but she'd find a way.

"Greetings of the evening, sister," the king said, eyeing Cami.

"Good evening, sir." She hoped she'd addressed him correctly. She didn't want to alienate him. If the king wanted Ray to marry someone else, maybe he'd help her get back home.

Sadira pulled away from Zedda and climbed up onto Cami's lap.

"Ah! You are in favor tonight," Zedda said, laughing. "One can never tell which lap a child will select."

Cami cuddled Sadira, delighted by the toddler's acceptance of her as one of the family. Even better, the king had addressed her as his sister, surely a good sign, regardless of what that hateful uncle Hamid had done. She started to relax, figuring that since this night was her last in Adnan, she'd better enjoy it.

Sadira's hair tickled Cami under the chin, making her chuckle. She asked the little girl, "Are you hungry, sweetie?" Picking up her fork, she fed Sadira a bite of lamb.

Watching, Rayhan's chest went tight. He hadn't heard Cami laugh for months. Tonight, she'd already giggled once or twice. And seeing her with his niece—he breathed deeply in an effort to dislodge the lump in his throat. Whether his wife knew it or not, she was born to bear children. His children.

Using a napkin Cami wiped a drop of gravy off Sadira's chin before feeding her more lamb. While the child chewed, his wife ate a few bites herself, then sipped some tea. "This is really wonderful. I love it here." She leaned back into her chair with a sigh that, to Rayhan's ears, seemed tinged with regret.

Rayhan started to sweat. He prayed that she hadn't meant her earlier threat to return to Texas on the morrow. He made a mental note to keep her safe in the palace.

"You do not miss your homeland?" Sharif asked.

Rayhan glared at his brother.

"Travel is always…interesting," Cami said smoothly. Her gaze slid over to the king.

"I apologize for the mode of your arrival," Kadar said, looking embarrassed.

Rayhan cut a glance to the king. Apologizing for anything wasn't like Kadar. A ruler in their father's mold, Kadar believed he could do no wrong. Perhaps his generosity of spirit this night was due to anxiety over Habiba, or maybe Kadar felt charitable because of Cami's advice on the OPEC offer.

Whatever the cause, Cami looked happier and his mother, ecstatic. Rayhan calmed. Perhaps his story would have a happy ending. He didn't know how, but he'd find a way to assure Cami of his commitment to her and their marriage.

Sadira squirmed out of Cami's lap and ran off, gabbling in Arabic. Rayhan turned to see what had seized his niece's attention.

He caught his wife's gaze. "Uncle Hamid is back."

"That's nice." Her voice was neutral.

"He has brought other visitors." Kadar arose. His gaze swept the newcomers, then shifted to Cami. "It is the Sheikh al-Qamra with his son and daughter. Yes, that is Matana, the Princess al-Qamra.''

"The al-Qamra, called the People of the Moon, are very important politically,'' Sharif said.

"Stop it, Sharif.'' Ray's tone was steely. Cami jerked with surprise. She'd never heard such cold anger from her husband before.

Sharif spread his hands. "Stop what, brother? I merely make an observation—''

"You seek to force me into a marriage that is not acceptable.'' Ray rested his hand on Cami's shoulder. "Perhaps you do not understand. This is my wife. I will take no other.''

"The al-Qamra must be brought into the mainstream of Adnani political life.'' The grand vizier eyed Cami.

"Fine. Why don't *you* marry Matana?'' Ray asked Sharif.

Sharif looked around as though searching for the nearest exit. "Oh, no. No. That girl and her interfering father are too much for me.''

"Ha. You wish to preserve your reputation as the globe-trotting playboy prince.'' Ray stood to face the king, his voice dripping with scorn. "And our brother Tariq continues to frolic in the mud with tanks and guns. But I am a man and a husband and will not permit further undermining of my marriage!'' He slapped his palm on the table.

Zedda patted his tense fingers, which relaxed. "You are right, my son. We shall have to find another way to placate the al-Qamra.''

Ray sat, as did the king, who said, "Perhaps a

string of your wonderful horses, Rayhan, will compensate for the loss of a prince."

"Or perhaps ten thousand dinarii." Ray winked at Cami, his good mood apparently restored.

She smiled, buoyed by his unequivocal support. "Why are the al-Qamra so powerful?"

"Not powerful," Zedda said. "Influential. They are among the last nomadic tribes of Adnan. Every six months they complete a circuit of our nation, walking from the desert across the mountain passes to the Bay of Syed. As they are great communicators, they spread news and have much effect on opinion."

"They could be described as…as…defiantly traditional." The king picked up his goblet and swirled the contents. "Sharif is right. They must be brought into the mainstream of Adnani life and into this millennium."

"I understand." Cami stood, drawing back her shoulders. "Ray, please introduce me to our guests."

He took Cami's hand and led her to the gate to greet their guests. She narrowed her eyes at Uncle Hamid, that snake. She'd bet her ranch that he'd deliberately brought her rival here just to bait her. By Hamid's side stalked another man. Dressed in brown robes, he wasn't as elderly as the mullah but appeared older than Ray and his brothers. Probably Sheikh al-Qamra. Bringing up the rear was a slight figure, a young man, in black. The son, she guessed.

And Matana, a small, delicately formed girl, clad in pearly white. As she drew back her hood, Cami could see that Matana was exquisite, with high cheekbones that reflected the moonlight, enormous dark eyes and full red lips.

Cami wanted to run all the way back to Texas. She remembered something Ray had said yesterday, when he'd criticized her body: "You'll be nice and round, like an Adnani girl." Matana epitomized the Adnani ideal of beauty. She was a nice, plump pigeon, ready for his plate…or for his bed. Sick with jealousy, Cami felt her stomach wrench.

Besides, Matana was the daughter of a sheikh, the woman Ray's family had selected for him. Regardless of what he'd said at the dinner table, it was Ray's duty to marry for political advantage.

Cami refused to share Ray, but Adnani law and custom allowed him to take Matana al-Qamra to wife, as well. And if the marriage would be good for Adnan, did Cami have the right to stand in his way?

Suddenly her husband was by her side, the warmth of his hand on her elbow. He leaned close. "Remember who you are," he whispered into her ear.

Breathing deeply, she forced her body to relax while straightening her spine and stretching to her full height. In the heeled gold sandals she'd purchased that day, she towered over little Matana, who tilted back her head to look at Cami.

Hamid introduced Matana as Prince Rayhan's fi-ancée, his voice edged with malicious glee. By her side, Cami sensed Ray stiffening.

"Former fiancée," he said, his tone icy. "May I present to you she who will be my only wife, Camille Ellison al-Rashad."

Cami turned her head and looked into her husband's eyes. He met her gaze without flinching, while giving her arm a comforting squeeze. The tension in her stomach loosened and fell away.

"Yes, as you well know, Uncle Hamid, since we talked earlier today," she said, smiling, even though she wanted to smack the cruel old man.

Matana, with a bewildered expression, looked around and met the gaze of the slight young man standing behind her. He bent his head toward her ear and spoke to her in rapid Arabic. Her eyes widened, and she skewered Hamid with an outraged glare from beneath her impossibly long lashes. If looks could kill, roast Hamid would be served at dinner along with the b'stila pie.

With a nervous gulp, Cami continued. "I am Prince Rayhan's wife and consort. I'm pleased to meet you, Matana, though I wish the circumstances weren't so awkward. No one informed you?"

Her brother again spoke before Matana said, "N-no," in hesitant, careful English. She pressed her lips together.

Cami loosened her arm from Ray's grip to take Matana's elbow. "I'm sorry," she said, her voice soft. "Now that your engagement is over, what are your plans?" She gently led Matana over to the buffet tables for a more private chat, with the young man following.

Rayhan wanted to pump his fist into the air and shout out an American-style cheer.

Smiling every second, his wife had coolly and calmly chopped off his uncle's political legs at the knee. Based on Matana's reaction, Rayhan believed that none of the al-Qamra would ever trust Hamid again. The People of the Moon maintained a nomadic lifestyle, so the word would spread, and in a few short weeks, Hamid would find his power and influence greatly reduced among all Adnani.

Sheikh al-Qamra didn't look any too happy, either. Rayhan's mother, no doubt responding to her impeccable political instincts, moved quickly to the sheikh's side.

Ray edged away, allowing his mother to work her magic. But he believed that even Zedda's smooth diplomacy couldn't alter the inevitable.

Though Cami had used a friendly tone of voice, Rayhan had seen the dangerous glitter in her eyes. He reflected that Hamid was most fortunate that Cami wasn't wearing cowboy boots. She looked as though she wanted to stomp on Hamid's toes for creating the situation. Rayhan was equally infuriated. What was the wily mullah's game?

It didn't matter. After glowering at his uncle, Rayhan looked for Cami. He hoped that he could quickly extricate his wife from the situation. With her help, he was sure he could untangle the thicket of emotions that had twisted his heart into confused knots. He desperately wanted to be alone with her.

Near the buffet table, Cami wore a supremely self-satisfied smile as she chatted with Prince al-Qamra, who'd translated for his sister. Cami offered him a plate and gestured to the buffet. A few steps away the king now played diplomat, no doubt exerting himself to soothe Princess al-Qamra's ill humor.

Rayhan eased his wife away from Prince al-Qamra, who bowed and nodded.

"You appear pleased with the world," Ray said to Cami.

She stuck her straight little nose into the air. "I think I'm quite good at this princess thing."

"I told you, you are perfect. Why do you doubt yourself, my wife?"

She nodded in Matana's direction. "Ray, Matana's a peach. Why'd you turn her down?"

He shrugged. "Oh, Matana's not a bad sort. But we have little in common. She doesn't speak English. She doesn't love Texas. And she's not you."

Her cheeks flushed a most charming shade of rose, visible in the lanterns lighting the courtyard.

"Shall we now retire?" He offered her his hand.

She stiffened, and didn't take it.

He sighed. "Cami. You do not understand. Most couples do not have what we have, my darling."

"What?" She didn't resist when he pulled her to his side.

He must have piqued her curiosity. "It is good between us. Very, very good. Think you any other man's touch would pleasure you so well?"

Cami looked at Ray. She had to admit, if only to herself, that even the slight caress of his fingers on hers as he escorted her to their suite was enough to thrill her to her toes and bring her to her knees...if she let that happen.

But she wouldn't.

Or would she? Her body quivered. Heat pooled in her belly.

He'd publicly claimed her as his only wife. He said she was perfect, describing her in complimentary terms to everyone he met. Although she'd filed for divorce, he refused to accept the death of their marriage, even though a lovely consort was available.

Ray opened the heavy, carved door to his—their—bedroom and ushered her inside, kissing her even before the door was partially open. He kicked the door shut while pulling her close.

She couldn't suppress her response to the tender brush of his mouth. When his fingers fumbled at the buttons securing her tunic, she didn't resist. She couldn't deny the excitement thrilling through her body. Everything that had happened—their blissful honeymoon followed by weeks of deprivation, then days of frustrating, unfulfilled closeness—had combined to stretch her control to the breaking point.

She wanted him.

She needed him.

She loved him.

Opening the halves of her garment, he exposed her naked breasts to the moonlight streaming into the room. He cupped and lifted them to his mouth, tonguing her nipples into ecstasy.

Ray raised his head. Her breasts, deprived of his warm caress, cooled, the tips hardening into stiff little nubs that ached for his love. She moaned with suppressed passion.

He feathered delicate kisses up her neck until he came to her ear. "Do you remember our first kiss?"

Sighing with remembered pleasure, she murmured, "Oh, yeah."

"And then later, when we again met at the pond."

She shivered in his arms.

"Like a river goddess, you walked out of the water and into my heart." His voice had dropped to an intimate whisper. "It was the most erotic moment of my life."

"Me, too. Not even our honeymoon—"

"I know. But our loving is so wonderful. Can we not try to find again the reasons we married?"

Spearing her fingers into his hair, Cami dragged him close for a long, deep kiss. His big hands dropped to her hips, kneading her buttocks through her clothes. The heat of his touch pervaded the layers of heavy silk, inflaming her desire.

While they kissed, he walked her over to his bed.

After they'd loved, Rayhan eased his weight off his wife and stared at the ceiling, trying to compose his disordered thoughts.

As usual, Cami quickly divined his mood. "What's up, Ray?" She stroked his side.

His flesh rippled with renewed need. He rolled to face her. "I have had many women. And yet, the act of love takes on a unique and magical quality with you. It has never been so good for me."

"Me, neither." She grinned at him.

"I think perhaps you do not understand how special this is because I was your first." He wove a strand of her hair around his fingers. "And, I pray, your last.

"But believe me, my Cami, when I say to you that the act of love is rarely so pleasurable. It is not common for a man and a woman to find paradise at the same moment. Yet you and I have climbed the heights together more than once. It is not only physical. It is because we are true mates."

Rayhan clasped her face in his hands, framing her cheeks with his palms. He became vividly aware of every aspect of his wife: her wide, wondering eyes, which masked her sharp intellect; the texture of her flushed skin; her lips, soft and sensual with their love-making.

He thought about everything they shared. Their love of horses. Their ranches in Texas, which would join, as they had, into one perfect whole. She had even developed a fondness for Adnan; had she not said she loved the place, despite the harshness of her treatment by some members of his family?

"You have captured my heart, seized my soul. Everything about you fascinates me," he said, his voice husky. "Your beautiful face, which shines with your inner light. Your mouth, which always, with complete honesty, reflects your feelings. Your lovely, strong body, which I hope will bear us many healthy children.

"When we were apart, the world turned gray and dead. When we are together—even when we argue— my world is brilliant again with color and light.

"I cannot happily live without you, my Camille. If that is not love, then what is it, this love you crave?"

Her exquisite eyes filled with tears. "You...you love me."

"Yes, my beloved. I love you. I am yours forever."

"That's all I needed to know," she whispered, slipping her arms around his neck.

"Then we will stay together?" Rayhan couldn't stop the choke of need in his voice. He didn't have to stop it. Cami was his true mate. She could see every flaw and still love him. He was sure of that.

"Together, forever."

"Forever."

Epilogue

One month later

His wheelchair pushed by one of the royal servants, Charles rolled down the ramp of the king's jet. By Cami's side, Ray chuckled. "Your father looks as though he had a much better flight than did you."

"Amelia Earhart had a better flight than mine." Cami pushed back her hood. The noontime sun of Syed beat down on her head, but she didn't care. She wanted her father to be able to spot her blond hair among all the dark Adnani.

Behind her, and to her right, scores of reporters, camera operators and onlookers clustered behind a yellow barrier patrolled by the local police. Since they'd announced their plans to renew their vows in a lavish public ceremony, Cami and Ray had been relentlessly shadowed by the press.

Now, the day before the rituals would begin, Adnani excitement had attained Himalayan heights. None of the royals could poke a nose outside the palace without a horde of media demanding interviews.

As minister without portfolio, Ray had decided that allowing full press access to certain events would quell the antiroyal, anti-American rumors. The arrival of Cami's father was the beginning of four days of media madness. Cami, gritting her back teeth when she heard the news, had resolved to grin and bear it.

Wearing a white *abaya* embroidered with the Adnani national colors, she stepped away from Ray's protective aura and advanced to the end of the ramp. She met her father and bent to kiss his cheek. "Hello, Daddy."

"Kiddo, I wouldn't have recognized you in that get-up except for your hair. You've gone native on me!"

Cami laughed, then edged aside to let Ray greet her father. Ray shook her dad's hand, saying, "Relax when I do this." He quickly kissed Charles on both cheeks in a traditional welcome.

Dad stared at Ray, Cami giggled, and the crowd erupted in cheers.

Hand in hand, Cami and Ray accompanied Charles to the king's limo. After they were comfortably seated, Cami asked, "So is it true? Have the two of you really buried the hatchet?"

Ray lounged against the cushions on the right side of the luxurious car. "You doubt my word, my princess?" His teasing smile belied the seriousness of the question.

"No, but—"

"Everything is fine." Her father patted her hand. "It was my fault, anyhow—"

"No, no." Ray poured orange juice into a glass and handed it to Cami. "The blame is entirely mine. I was a fool—"

"I was a cheat." Charles's tone was somber. "We were looking at some tough times, Cami, and I couldn't bear for you to go without. But I was ashamed of what I'd done for the next ten years."

"That is all over, is it not?" Ray asked.

"If you can forgive me, it is." Charles extended his right hand to Ray, who took it, smiling.

Three days later, as Cami sat next to Ray at a banqueting table, she said to him, "I think we're well and truly married."

"Yes, and do not ever forget it, my wife." Lifting her hand, he kissed her wedding ring.

Because of the diverse religious groups in Adnan, their wedding lasted three days and included three ceremonies, Islamic, Christian and Jewish. Protocol required them to attend scores of parties all over Syed from dusk until dawn.

Finally Cami, dressed in a traditional white dress— her twelfth gown of the three-day period—had circled Ray seven times, part of the ancient Jewish ceremony, the last of the wedding rites. The feast that followed, attended by numerous international leaders, lasted until midnight.

Cami nibbled on a stuffed grape leaf, trying to enjoy herself, though she was exhausted by the countless social gatherings. She wondered if she'd ever return to her beloved ranch again.

Pushing aside her homesickness, she counted her blessings. Not only did Ray adore her, but the men in her life—her father and her husband—seemed to be getting along famously.

Cami looked across the table at her father. Resplendent in a tuxedo, with servants waiting on him day and night, Charles appeared to be having the time of his life. The palace children had adopted him as a kind of surrogate grandfather. He delighted in teaching them how to play poker and checkers.

Beside her Ray put his hand on her knee under the table and squeezed. "This has all been very much fun, but when are we going back home?"

She turned to him, smiling. Did he mean what she hoped? "Home?"

"Yes, home. To Texas. I am—how do you say it? Housesick for my ranch, my home and my horses. Do you not miss your Sugar?"

Her amazing husband had virtually echoed her thoughts. "Oh, Ray!" She flung her arms around his neck. "Let's leave tomorrow."

He laughed. "If that is your wish."

"But what about your job?"

"Minister without portfolio? I'll resign."

"But you always wanted a high government post."

He shrugged. "It is less than it is supposed to be. I have already discussed the matter with Kadar. He agrees to appoint me—us—as special envoys to the United States in regard to oil. It will be our responsibility to manage the oil trade between Adnan and the United States."

"Hmm." Cami sipped mint tea. "That sounds... interesting. We'd have to shuttle back and forth from Texas."

"Yes, with visits to Washington, D.C. So how about it?" He took her hands in his.

A score of flashbulbs popped as the media immortalized the moment. Cami winced, but Ray appeared oblivious. He continued, "Will you share this crazy life with me, my wife?"

"Hmm." She fiddled with her wedding ring, pretending to mull over his proposition. "There's only one problem."

His face fell. "What is it? Tell me. You know that together, we will solve our problems. True love overcomes all obstacles, does it not?"

"Yes, it does." Cami smiled. Never had she such confidence in her husband's devotion. Since that wonderful night when he'd openly declared his love for her, their marriage had strengthened, growing strong enough to endure any adversity life might cast at them. "We'll just have to be careful about the planes we choose. I'm told that flying in unpressurized cabins is bad for pregnant women."

Ray drew in his breath in an audible gasp. "Do you mean—"

"Yes, I do." Cami adored the expression of joy and pride on her husband's face. She drew his head down to hers for a passionate kiss. "Consider our baby another wedding present."

* * * * *

MILLS & BOON®

Live the emotion

Modern
romance™

BOUGHT FOR THE MARRIAGE BED
by Melanie Milburne

Nina will do anything to keep her twin's baby from harm.
So when Marc Marcello wants to take his brother's child,
Nina lets herself be bought as Marc's bride instead. But
what price can be placed on her...in his bed?

THE ITALIAN'S WEDDING ULTIMATUM
by Kim Lawrence

Alessandro Di Livio always protects his family, even
seducing gold digging Sam Maguire to keep her away from
his brother-in-law! But when passion leads to pregnancy,
Alessandro wants to keep Sam as his wife – and their baby
as his heir!

THE INNOCENT VIRGIN *by Carole Mortimer*

Abby Freeman is thrilled when she gets a job as a TV chat
show host, and who better to grill than famous journalist
Max Harding? Max is happy to let Abby get close – but
only in private. How can Abby get the story...without
losing her innocence?

RUTHLESS REUNION *by Elizabeth Power*

Sanchia has amnesia but when Alex Sabre recognises her,
she realises they once knew each other intimately. To
unlock her past Sanchia must spend time with Alex. What
happens when she learns the truth about the man she's
falling in love with...again?

On sale 5th May 2006

Available at WHSmith, Tesco, ASDA, Borders, Eason,
Sainsbury's and most bookshops

www.millsandboon.co.uk

0406/01b

0406/05a

MILLS & BOON®

Live the emotion

In May 2006, By Request presents two
collections of three favourite romances by
our bestselling Mills & Boon authors:

Australian
Playboy
Tycoons

by **Miranda Lee**
The Playboy's Proposition
The Playboy's Virgin
The Playboy in Pursuit

Make sure you buy these
irresistible stories!

On sale 5th May 2006

MILLS & BOON®

Live the emotion

Convenient Weddings

A Husband of Convenience
by Jacqueline Baird
A Passionate Surrender by Helen Bianchin
Bride for a Year by Kathryn Ross

Make sure you buy these irresistible stories!

On sale 5th May 2006

Available at WHSmith, Tesco, ASDA, Borders, Eason, Sainsbury's and most bookshops

www.millsandboon.co.uk

4 FREE

BOOKS AND A SURPRISE GIFT!

We would like to take this opportunity to thank you for reading this Mills & Boon® book by offering you the chance to take FOUR more specially selected titles from the Modern Romance™ series absolutely FREE! We're also making this offer to introduce you to the benefits of the Reader Service™—

- ★ **FREE home delivery**
- ★ **FREE gifts and competitions**
- ★ **FREE monthly Newsletter**
- ★ **Exclusive Reader Service offers**
- ★ **Books available before they're in the shops**

Accepting these FREE books and gift places you under no obligation to buy, you may cancel at any time, even after receiving your free shipment. Simply complete your details below and return the entire page to the address below. You don't even need a stamp!

YES! Please send me 4 free Modern Romance books and a surprise gift. I understand that unless you hear from me, I will receive 6 superb new titles every month for just £2.80 each, postage and packing free. I am under no obligation to purchase any books and may cancel my subscription at any time. The free books and gift will be mine to keep in any case.

P6ZED

Ms/Mrs/Miss/Mr ....Initials ....
BLOCK CAPITALS PLEASE

Surname ....

Address ....

....

....Postcode........................

Send this whole page to:
UK: FREEPOST CN81, Croydon, CR9 3WZ